Mallard

Spies, Speed and Murder

ANDY LYNCH

"Spies and steam trains, intrigue and speed, what more does a cracking good story need?"

Frank Cottrell-Boyce, Screenwriter

"Mallard: Spies, Speed and Murder is an absolute corker of a tale! Set during the lead-up to WWII, the Brits are engineering the fastest train on Earth – and the Nazis will stop at nothing to destroy it in this captivating spy thriller"

Amy Burgwin, Endeavour Media

© Andy Lynch 2018

Andy Lynch has asserted his rights under the Copyright, Design and Patents Act, 1988, to be identified as the author of this work.

First published in 2018 by Endeavour Media Ltd.

For Frances B. Lynch 1948 - 2018
My wife.

ONE

Berlin, Germany, late May 1938

It was a cloudless sky. The bright sun smiled down on people enjoying pavement cafés and bars. Bands played, and occasional spontaneous dancers intermingled with the shoppers and the workers. Government buildings were adorned with huge black and red flags fluttering in a light breeze; it was a modern city looking forward to the promise of a glorious future – the capital of a country made great again by a charismatic and beloved man. Life was good.

In a large house two tram stops from the carefree Kurfürstendamm, Helena wiped away tears and opened the heavy oak door into her father's study, hiding how upset she had been helping Erna pack her few precious possessions. Jacob Rosenhoff rose from his desk to greet her, still holding the letter he had been reading.

"Erna is leaving now and she would like to say goodbye papa." Helena said, trying bravely to force a smile.

"Of course," he replied. He put the letter down. They stepped into the hallway where Erna was standing with her small canvas suitcase.

She had a childlike vulnerability as she looked for a last time at things she had dusted and polished with such care and satisfaction. The pair of Chinese vases, the bronze bust, the shiny wooden coat-stand that needed just the flick of a duster to make it gleam. Her grey winter coat was incongruous in the spring sunshine. But it had to be taken somehow and was easier to wear than carry.

Erna had rehearsed the speech she was about to make: to tell the Rosenhoffs how happy she had been to work for them for the past four years; how she had appreciated their gift of money, overall kindness and their care; how she had learned from their informal tutoring; how she had felt more family than employee.

It remained unsaid. The moment she started speaking she burst into tears, as did Helena. All three knew they were unlikely to ever meet again.

Mrs Rosenhoff had died soon after Erna had taken up her position in the household, so she had bonded naturally with Helena, having lost her own mother at an early age. They were more like cousins than mistress and servant, but as life in Berlin had become increasingly intolerable for Jews like Erna, she had forced herself to look forward. Soon she was to escape Germany completely for a new life in America, and today in fact would brave the dangers of the city streets to meet with her fiancé.

The speech could not be made. It was impossible. But Erna, through her tears, promised herself that everything she had failed to say would be in the letter she would write soon to Helena Rosenhoff and her father – the beloved family she had been so much at home with.

Doncaster, Yorkshire

Hot here, as well, if not as hot as Berlin eight hundred miles away. Two men in their early twenties, Sam Bolton and Edgar Travis, carried their jackets as they walked down a terraced street, although their caps and waistcoats remained inflexibly in place. It was a customary start to their working day, and geography dictated it was always Sam who called at Edgar's, where Mrs Travis would offer tea and toast, irking his own mother as he always left her kitchen well fed. She'd become more sensitive of late because the two families were now connected by marriage.

"And suppose you fall off the rotten thing?" Edgar was saying. "I'll get the blame."

"I'm not going to fall off. If you just make sure it's fit on right." Sam replied. They were heading for Doncaster Railway Works, better known as The Plant, where both had been apprenticed. But Sam had qualified as a draughtsman, while Edgar was still a fitter.

"It sounded a right stupid idea to me," said Edgar. "Right from the start."

"Aye, and that's because you're just a fitter," Sam kidded. "I don't know why we're even talking about it – you've got to do it on my say so."

"It's just an excuse for you to get out of the drawing office, if you ask me. Another step up above your bloody station."

"But no one's asking, are they? I've got the brains and you've got the tools. Just do as you're told."

"Bloody cheek," laughed Edgar. "Just make sure you're fastened on tight that's all, or I'll never hear the last of it from our Gwen and your mother."

The railway works was huge, dominating the area both in size and importance for the town. It offered both of them a secure job for life, and for Sam a ladder to accomplish his ambitions. He had left school at only fourteen, but had worked his way up from apprentice fitter to the drawing office, and was now part of a team responsible for designing new locomotives and improving the performance of existing ones. All worked under the guidance of chief design engineer, Sir Nigel Gresley.

The goal, the ultimate, was the world speed record for a railway locomotive. With many fearing a war with Germany was a growing possibility, Sir Nigel Gresley was determined that the crown should be

Britain's. The Germans, and Herr Hitler, saw diesel engines as the future, but Gresley and his faithful acolytes would prove that they were wrong.

In their hearts and souls, they believed – they knew – that steam was king, now and forever.

After the brothers-in-law had clocked in, and shared some banter with their friends, Sam walked the few hundred yards to the shunting sheds. Because of the dangerous operation he had agreed to undertake to help Sir Nigel, some of the younger draughtsmen had 'got up' a little skit, which they gathered round to make Sam watch.

It was a mock funeral, with solemn eulogies read out from scrolls, and many eyes ostentatiously wiped to mark his sad demise. It did not last long, because some of the older foremen put a stop to it, on grounds of bad taste. It was, they said, bad luck. A harbinger of doom.

Sam Bolton joined in the scorn felt by the younger men. But he could tell the story later, when the family met for their usual Monday tea. Sam and his younger sister Edith still lived in their parents' tiny terraced home. Older sister Gwen shared a home with Mrs Travis since she'd married Edgar. The tea-date was always Monday – washday – because it meant Gwen could pick up her laundry, which her mother had volunteered to do until the couple "got on their feet." It also ensured that she visited her old home at least once a week. Mrs Bolton was not yet ready to cut the apron strings …

Max and Bruno Schafer were not identical, but they were clearly twins. Big burly farm boys, labourers, with less intelligence than their livestock. They were also killers.

In the spring sunshine, they looked at the body with very little interest. She was young and small, and wore a large winter coat despite the heat, but so what? She had also clung with total desperation to her canvas suitcase that, on inspection, had held nothing of the slightest value. They had pocketed the cash found in the inner coat pocket.

She had been waiting for someone when they'd spotted her, and her heavy coat had been unbuttoned.

"Jewess," said Max. He had pointed to the necklace she was wearing, which marked her out. To the pathological twins, keen to prove their worth to a barbaric ruling party, Erna had chosen herself … to be their latest victim.

TWO

Above a Berlin bar a naked fat man flushed the toilet and looked at himself in the mirror as he washed his hands. He saw a podgy face mottled red by high blood pressure, baggy eyes, receding hairline and double chin above a bulging neck – the products of unfettered over-indulgence.

Vernon Stainton, though, was thoroughly content. He waddled from the toilet down a short corridor to his bedroom, where the sunshine lit both his double bed and his mistress, Herta, in a white cotton nightdress that barely contained her. She was holding a black notebook, a telegram and a pencil as Vernon climbed back into bed. Although he would have liked another hour's rest, she was concentrating.

"Vernon, it says down here a brewery has taken over. Is that good English? What does it mean? What brewery."

Vernon sighed. "It means I'm working for a different set of people," he said wearily. "It's all so bloody tedious."

"And this word?"

Vernon took the paper and found it with his

finger.

"'Seconded'," he read.

"Which means?" She was looking seriously puzzled. Herta's native tongue was German.

"I've been drafted into another department. Or as the clowns back in Blighty insist on putting it, a rival brewery has taken over."

"Why that is in code?"

He shook his head slowly. "They're just like bloody kids."

Herta read the telegram again and referred back to Vernon's codebook. He could not relax knowing she would soon ask what another word meant. He was willing her to get up and make them both coffee but was resigned to probably having to do it himself. He would give her five more minutes.

In The Plant, Sam was met by the inspector in charge of safety, who was nervous about what was about to happen. It had been Sam's idea, designed to sort out a

technical fault on the new engine tender, and to the official it seemed fraught with danger.

They chatted as they walked to the gigantic doors of the railway sheds, and Sam's heart also quickened as they stepped inside. Not with nerves, though, but excitement. The waiting engine was a truly heart-stopping sight. Barely three months old, in a shining livery of garter blue, already fired up to a full 250 lbs boiler pressure, it was a massive creature yearning to be set free. Although Sam had only played a minor part in its development and construction, he felt that he might burst with pride. Breathing in the pungent odours that filled the vast shed, odours of smoke, steam, hot oil, soot, grease and coal, he loved every atom of it. *Mallard* was a work of art.

He and the inspector walked to the rear of *Mallard*, passing a driver and his fireman waiting on the footplate. Arriving at the coupled tender, Sam spotted Edgar crammed underneath it securing a makeshift wooden platform with metal straps and bolts. For the moment, they forgot their usual banter. The work was all but finished, and Edgar invited him to squirm down and inspect. Within seconds, lying on the track between the tender's wheels, Sam declared elatedly: "The job's a good'un!"

"Aye," said his brother-in-law, drily. "As good as it'll ever be, no danger. It's champion."

The inspector, staring into the oily, reeking space, was not so sure. Not so much at the job that Edgar had done, but the wisdom of the "whole damn exercise." Was Sam Bolton really intending to travel at high speed underneath this massive engine strapped to a raft of rickety wood and leather? Was the young man mad?

"Nay," said Edgar, "he'll be all reet, ah promise thee. Where there's no sense there's no feeling. And if he comes back dead his sister, my wife'll bloody skin me alive. Plus, he's got this clobber to keep him safe. He'll be like a knight in shining armour!"

The "clobber" was an oilskin coat and sou'wester, which Sam climbed into sheepishly, thinking he must look "a proper fool." As he wormed himself onto the platform, Edgar added brusquely, "It won't shift, lad, ah promise thee. Just be bloody careful and 'ang on tight for Gwen."

"I will, Edgar" Sam replied. "Don't fret" And they exchanged a look of real affection.

THREE

In his cluttered office across The Plant, Sir Nigel Gresley acknowledged his secretary's message over the intercom with some dismay. His London visitor had arrived, and he was not looking forward to the meeting at all. His written replies to detailed questions had been deemed inadequate, and Sir Harry Trafford had insisted on making the long journey from London up to Doncaster to speak in person.

He was a retired artillery officer from the Great War, now heading one of the obscure intelligence agencies that were springing up like mushrooms in the current climate of military unease. Herr Hitler's fault. Herr Hitler, thought Sir Nigel grouchily, was a royal pain.

Despite the fact that Trafford had chosen to travel by car not rail, which Gresley also found strangely irksome, the two soon discovered common ground. His department, it turned out, specialised in assessing Germany's transportation infrastructure, which was being massively extended and modernised under the Third Reich. Hitler was pouring money into it, while Britain …

"In short," he said, "our myopic Civil Service

seems to think that we can live on air. They're starving us, Sir Nigel. And at this time of all times, I need to validate and expand my team. Transport, sir, is vital. Vital!"

Sir Nigel soon decided the short and tubby visitor was brusque and efficient rather than arrogant, and had impressive areas of expertise beyond mere weaponry. They respected each other's fields, both were realistic about the growing industrial power of the Third Reich, and both were fierce patriots.

"Frankly," said Trafford, "there are many men in Government who believe there's a real possibility of war between the two of us, while others are confident Hitler's ambitions stop well short of all-out conflict."

"And you?"

"Well, he introduced conscription in '36, which was specifically forbidden, as you know, and some of the smarter heads in Whitehall have known damn well that there's been secret rearmament going on since '33 at least. And now it's '38. Twenty years since the last dust-up."

"And if the balloon does go up, transport will be the key. Obviously." They shared a smile.

"And if we're to beat them," Sir Harry said, "detailed knowledge of their transport infrastructure's an essential tool. You went there in June 1934 according to my records, to study diesel locomotives in Hamburg. We think that you're the man to ask."

"But as I told you in my letters, my knowledge could be well out of date by now. The Third Reich doesn't hang about, does it? Modernisation seems to be fundamental to their creed."

Trafford nodded.

"You suggested a new ground study, a very detailed study, was the way forward. And you said you were too busy to take it on yourself."

Sir Nigel laughed.

"Without wishing to sound too arrogant, I also suggested I might be too well known to undertake the task. I could hardly go inspecting the new top diesels and the signalling infrastructure without being spotted. I have appeared in several newspaper articles."

He had explained all this in his letters, and Sir Harry had, in fact, taken it on board. Sir Nigel had suggested one of his draughtsman engineers as being the ideal man for the task, and guessed, irascibly, that Sam Bolton had been dismissed out of hand by the snooty London brass. Not so.

"This man, Sam Bolton, that you put forward. Have you spoken to him about the idea?" Trafford asked.

"Ah, so you are interested in him?"

"That's why I'm here, Sir Nigel – I read between the lines. This young man sounds right up my street.

I came up all this way because I want to meet him. I take it he's available?"

"Yes, he is. I've sounded him out about it already, and he jumped at the chance. He's done discreet surveillance for me several times."

Sir Harry looked puzzled and Sir Nigel knew that an explanation was necessary. "We'll go and find him and I'll explain as we walk. Be prepared for a shock by the way."

Sir Harry was highly intrigued and looked forward to meeting Sir Nigel's nominee.

FOUR

Above the Berlin bar, Herta had persisted in decoding Vernon's telegram, forcing him from his bed and into making coffee. He cut a barrel-like figure in the small kitchen, with his braces outside his vest supporting large, baggy trousers, and his bare feet sticking to the linoleum. Herta appeared at the door in her nightdress, telegram and codebook both still in hand.

"What is transpitter? This word transpitter?"

Vernon sat heavily at the kitchen table.

"You're not supposed to read any of this you know," he said.

"It's good for my English. Transpitter?" She sat down next to him.

"It's probably transmitter. Oh God, I hope they're not wanting me to start using a bloody radio. Over and out and suchlike tedious nonsense."

The bar was due for opening in a couple of hours, and as usual he had drunk too much the night before. All he wanted was strong coffee, a cigarette, and perhaps a brandy to fuel him to start the day. And here was Herta mithering about some 'schoolboy' message from London.

"Wait a minute." He checked her notes. "It's

trainspotter, not bloody transpitter. Trainspotter."

"So? And what is that?"

"It means not only have I been seconded, I've been bloody scuppered." said Vernon in disgust. "It'll be some bloody kid fresh from university's latest wheeze. Place is bloody full of them."

She brushed blonde hair out of her eyes and gave him a curious look.

"Scuppered. What is bloody scuppered?"

"Bloody scuppered means bloody buggered. Up the creek without a bloody paddle. And a bloody sight more."

"This bloody English is so bloody difficult. Why such a bloody mood?" Now she was laughing at him, but at least she was standing up to make the coffee. Vernon softened. He decoded the rest of the message himself.

"Bad mood because my new brewery's sending a trainspotter to come and stay with me."

"And what is a trainspotter?" Herta asked. "You did not said … say."

She gave him the coffee, but Vernon now needed more. He pointed to a cupboard. She took out a bottle of brandy and handed it over. He added a generous measure into his steaming mug.

"Somebody who likes to look at trains," he said.

"This one likes to look at German trains."

"And who will that be?"

Vernon drained his mug, and reached for the bottle.

"I don't know, but he'll be arriving very soon. A bloody guest staying with me for weeks and weeks. The bloody cheek of it."

He sat back on his kitchen chair and lit a cigarette.

"Don't say a bloody word to anyone, understood? Not a bleeding bloody word." Herta grinned.

"Kein Wort. Kein blutig Word. Oh lord and master …"

If Vernon Stainton could have seen his "bloody trainspotter" at that very moment, the "bloody cheek of it" would have driven him distracted. Sam Bolton was standing beside the quietly steaming *Mallard* outside the railway shed at Doncaster, looking nothing like a dangerous spy at all.

Resplendent in oilskins and sou'wester – dripping wet and caked with stinking grease – he was explaining to a group of men including Edgar exactly what he'd seen while thundering at high speed strapped to his pallet underneath the locomotive's tender.

When one of the excited group pointed out two approaching men, they suddenly fell into embarrassed silence. It was Sir Nigel Gresley and an equally impressive stranger. And all of his workforce, every last employee of the LNER, held their chief in awe.

Sir Nigel was a quietly-spoken man who rarely needed to raise his voice. Hiding his amusement at Sam's appearance, he said simply: "You survived, young man? Good."

"Yes sir," Sam said. "I did."

"And was your adventure productive?" Sir Nigel asked.

Sam smiled through his mask of grease and soot.

"Very much so, Sir. I'm sure now that it is the design of the scoop."

"As you suggested to me earlier," Sir Nigel replied. "I'll look forward to reading your report." He turned to the other gentleman, and the workers moved back slightly. "This is the young man I've been telling you about, Harry."

Sir Harry Trafford drew on his newly-lit pipe and weighed Sam up through the aromatic smoke. The young draughtsman cut a strange figure in his mackintosh and sailor's headgear, and Sir Harry decided it would be inappropriate to shake his wet and grimy hand. But he smiled, and Sam smiled back. Both sensed it was the start of something good.

"Should we remove the platform now, sir?" Edgar enquired.

"No," Sir Nigel said. "Leave it attached if you

think it's safe. We'll be brake testing soon and it might prove rather useful. What do you think, young man?"

"I'd say Edgar did a grand job, sir. As long as anyone who goes on it watches how the brake cylinders tip forward when they're applied it's safe as houses."

"Good. We'll leave it for now then, and well done everybody. You get yourself cleaned up, young Bolton, and come to my office. Sir Harry here would like to have a word with you. And everybody – thank you for all your efforts this morning."

On their walk from his office Sir Nigel had explained to the London visitor what Sam had been trying to find out. There was a recurring problem of water getting into the axle boxes on A4 Pacific loco tenders, and he had taken it on himself to find out why. Underneath the tender, he had discovered, the device that scooped up water for the boiler from a trough between the rails formed a wave that defeated the seals.

Sam felt confident a vertical plate welded into the scoop to split the water and decrease the pressure build-up would easily do the trick. Sir Nigel nodded, pleased.

Sir Harry was impressed by Sam, and intrigued to learn that he already had experience in a form of spying. Gathering information by fair means or foul was rife between competing railway companies, because speed and efficiency meant prestige and honour, which translated into increased revenue and which, naturally, in turn resulted in higher returns for shareholders, greater investment and continuing success.

Sam, level-headed and courageous, had more than once winkled out secret information from the opposition that had affected the design of a new engine or modified an existing boiler.

"And he is in no way foolhardy," Sir Nigel told Sir Harry. "In my view, he's the ideal man for you, and I'm sure he'd find secondment to the government right up his street. What young man wouldn't? To get free railway travel throughout Germany – and to be a spy!"

FIVE

Helena Rosinhoff arrived with a cup of tea for her father. It was the first time she had done it since Erna had left, but neither commented on her departure for fear of renewed tears. A year ago, they had shared her happiness about her engagement to a young man with an extended family in America, and the possibility of a new life in another world. Both knew Erna would be better off, but it did not stop the worry and the loss.

Jacob Rosenhoff had been a successful businessman until his factory had been abruptly taken from him and transferred to an 'Aryan' competitor. There was no compensation, and the family was forced to sell off anything they could just to survive. Although he'd done his best to protect daughter Helena from the harsh realities, she was all too well aware of how – and why – their comfortable world was shrinking.

Jacob had also been a community spokesperson who had met and tried to reason with the strengthening ruling party since its rise to power. But many Jews had fled the country, and he knew he'd stayed too long. He and Helena were trapped and their lives were becoming a nightmare. He took a sip of tea, and touched a letter on his desk.

"My friend Ibram has written from New York," he said. "He apologises for the short notice but he wanted to give me definite news rather than speculation. There's going to be a multi-nation conference in Évian-les-Bains, in France, to discuss the refugee situation and what each country can do about it. President Roosevelt himself has instigated it, and Ibram is urging me to attend. To speak first-hand about our situation here in Berlin."

"You must attend," said Helena. "Father, you must attend. But will they … will you be allowed to travel?"

He nodded sombrely.

"Perhaps they will encourage me," he said. "Encourage me to leave, to get rid of me. Perhaps they will provide transport for me to travel there."

He was not speaking seriously, they both knew. His daughter managed a small smile.

"An optimistic thought," she said. She watched him sip his tea, with desperate sadness. Not long before a proud businessman with an active social life, he now seemed much older than his years. His wife's death had been a terrible blow, but they had supported each other and survived, with Erna's help. Now there seemed little left and speculation about the future merely led to misery. They lived each day as it came and the letter from New York was a rare fillip.

Rosenhoff picked it up once more.

"But Erna, dear Erna, did receive her visa for America at last," he said, "and, please God, this conference will lead to many, many more. I must attend, I will attend, and you must come with me of course."

They both sat silently. And hoped that there might be a way.

In Doncaster, Sam Bolton's fourteen-year-old sister Edith could hardly keep her mind on laying the table and keeping an eye on the simmering vegetables. She had a secret, and she couldn't wait for her mother to get back from seeing grandma, who lived in the next street. Mealtime conversation was usually sport or railway, but Edith had a subject to top everything. It might even be the talk of all the neighbours when they found out.

Sam's mother ran the house on a tight timetable, with meals determined by what day of the week it was, and they rarely varied. Today was Monday so it was lamb saved from yesterday's roast, with fresh veg. Apples were free and abundant, so a pie would follow with homemade custard. Mother, expecting the usual routine returning from her visit, got instead an excited gabble.

"You'll never guess, mam!" Edith said. "Course you won't! How could you? It's the most amazing news!"

Mother was unimpressed.

"Edith, whatever is the matter with you? I hope those spuds aren't boiled dry."

"Of course not! When have I ever neglected anything?"

"Whenever you behave as giddy as this, my girl." She smiled. "Well come on then. Out with it!"

Edith took a deep breath, grinned – and then announced it.

"Our Sam's going to London! In the morning! No, not tomorrow, the day after! London!"

"Don't be silly, Edith."

"But he is, mam! He told me so! He wasn't kidding. He was serious. Ever so serious."

Her mother was dismissive. "He's going to work day after tomorrow. As usual. Sam always goes to work, whatever are you talking about?"

"He's told me."

"He's not due home yet. You can't have seen him."

"He's been and gone."

"Gone where?"

Edith shook her head vigorously. Her mam could be so frustrating!

"To tell Eric Bannister he'll be missing cricket. Not just practice night, but the match on Saturday as well. And that's not all. It doesn't stop at London."

When Sam returned, the family were gathering

for tea. His mother told him off for cutting it so fine, then Edith held them up some more with her announcement that Sam had news for them. Sister Gwen squeaked out her hope that he was about to announce his engagement, then blushed scarlet when the fact he wasn't even courting occurred to her.

When order was restored, Sam told his parents, sisters and brother-in-law of the extraordinary events of the day. That a government official had asked him if he'd go to Germany. That they wanted him to travel the railway system, and report back daily to an Englishman in Berlin who would be his host for four weeks.

"Host?" said his father Neville, who was also a railwayman of course. "You mean a spy, don't you? Ruddy hell, Sam, you're going to be a bloody spy!'

"Language!" said his mother, automatically. And Edith giggled.

Edgar's first reaction was to hope that he could now move up the batting order into Sam's position at third wicket down. His mother quickly came up with a list of questions starting with "Why you?" and ending up "Why you?" Then she went on to where her son would stay, what he would eat, who would do his laundering, what company he'd be keeping, and "You just make sure you write home every day, my lad!"

When dad could get a word in he asked about wages and overtime, if Sir Nigel had approved, and would he need a passport? Gwen said that if he ever went near Dresden could he bring her home a plate or two, because she'd heard that porcelain from there was very nice.

Sam, overwhelmed, held his hands up to ward off the barrage, and tormented Edgar by saying he'd been chosen because he was the cleverest and best-looking draughtsman in the office, and a "fantastic advert for the LNER in Germany." Edgar quipped it was because he'd not be missed in working hours, and that lying on his back relaxing underneath an A4 tender was the closest he would ever get to real work, and getting dirt on his girlie little hands.

"I'll be living in a bar, apparently," said Sam. 'That's what upsets you, Edgar, isn't it?" Which cost him much more time reassuring his mother and his sisters that he was completely capable of eating properly, seeing to his washing and ironing, and staying sober.

"He's a man called Victor Stainton who's my sort of manager," he said, "and his bar is on the Kurfürstendamm. And that's all I know."

"That doesn't surprise me" Edgar chirped in.

"Well you'll need to learn a lot more. It's not the same as over here you know, over there." Dad said, still reeling from the news.

"I'll be starting from London. People there'll tell

me all I need to know."

When the questions had dried up, they all enjoyed their meal, and the women did the washing up while the men went back to talk of cricket, trains and football. They cared little about the political situation in Europe, beyond agreeing that war was passingly remote. Germany was very good on locomotives, although their obsession with diesel was a shade short-sighted, and if it wanted to reoccupy bits of other countries it used to own, was that so very terrible?

Great Britain, thank God, need not get involved and Sam, whichever way you looked at it, was going to have the time of his life.

SIX

Bruno cooked the lunch today, because it was his turn.

It was a simple affair, consisting of boiled potatoes, left-over ham and cabbage, made simpler by the fact that it was what he always cooked, although every other day the ham had to be boiled from scratch.

It was the meal his mother had taught him, just the week before he and Max had left their home in Bavaria to travel to the capital to realise their dream. She'd taught his twin a basic soup with flour and dumplings, although he could almost bake bread as well. Almost, because it was only just edible. He needed much more practice.

Frau Schafer, however, was confident that she'd equipped her hefty sons with enough culinary knowledge not to starve, and was happy to have them leave the family home, where they were the biggest eaters and the smallest workers. She and her husband had four more sons and two daughters still dependent on them, so Bruno and Max had promised to send money home.

Which would be very much appreciated. When it

arrived.

After Max and Bruno had eaten, they planned to learn more of the speech they had obtained a copy of. Then they would go to the bar to meet the party official who had befriended them, and impress him with their new-found knowledge.

And the news of their latest killing, of which they were inordinately proud.

Erna, the little Jewish servant girl, had been their third victim.

Sam had been told to inform his colleagues he was going on a course at the LNER offices in Stratford, East London, and be vague about the details. His workmates expressed little surprise at this and showed no resentment. He was a popular member of the team, and it was widely acknowledged he would one day be promoted over them.

He left his house after an especially large breakfast, forced on him because his mother reasoned he did not know when he might eat again or what quality the food might be. It did not occur to her she'd packed enough 'home cooking' in his suitcase to supply his next three meals.

His father had left early for work, so had given his best wishes and advice the night before. The main thrust was not to get into any foolish arguments about football, as foreign teams were inferior and their supporters volatile. Unnecessary to mention cricket, as Germans would not know what it was.

Edith said her goodbyes before she left for school, while his mam refused to go to the station with him in case she made a fool of herself by crying on the platform. But she did make sure her son promised most solemnly to eat, write, bathe, launder and behave in the manner she had brought him up.

Sam departed from Doncaster Central at 9.06, seven minutes late due to some unexplained mishap further up the line, arriving at King's Cross about seven hours later. He was struck by how busy the station was with freight as well as passengers, which brought home how dependent the capital was on goods from the rest of Britain. He had seen hundreds of wagons carrying coal for the power stations, without which the city would grind to a halt. This made him think about Germany and its own dependence on energy. He would have to ask Mr Stainton if coal movements, as well as armaments, should be observed and recorded.

As instructed, he made his way to The Great Northern Hotel, which adjoined the station as part of the London North Eastern Railway company's services to travellers. He had a view encompassing swathes of track and rolling stock, which suited him just fine.

As there was plenty of daylight left, he thought

he might see a sight or two. Fancying a pie and pint, he found a pub called The Albany, where he ordered a steak and ale pie – excellent – and a pint of disappointing bitter. He also overheard, without meaning to, four men arguing. Their subject was the growing turmoil on the continent.

"The country's full up to bursting," one man was almost shouting. "We've masses of the unemployed already, and we can't take any more. So the Jews don't like the Nazis, well so what? We can't let them in, not even a few of them. England's our country, end of story."

Another man beside him violently agreed. Veins on his neck and cheeks were standing out, his face was almost purple.

"If we let a few in, then what happens? The trickle gets to be a stream, the stream grows to a flood, in no time we'd be swamped. We're full! Masses of unemployed already, and the refugees'd take what jobs are left. They'd work for next to nothing and drive wages down for all the rest of us."

"Dead right!" the first man said. "And they won't be satisfied until they've got rid of our religion and replaced it with their own. They wear funny clothes. They've all got beards! It's a well-known fact that Jews pollute the Christian bloodline."

Whatever facts and figures another man offered, those men would not be swayed. The man whose veins were fit to burst held his views immovably, and ended up suggesting that foreigners already here should be sent back where they came from. Sam, aware he had no statistics he could rely on, dared not intervene, although he was sure the man was very wrong. He did not know any Jewish people personally but had been taught at school about some of them being driven out of Russia and settling in Leeds. True, some of them did look rather strange, but they were clever, and worked extremely hard.

As to the argument that the country was full up, Sam wondered if this man had ever travelled outside London. If he had, he would have seen mile upon mile of free open space, and not all taken up by farming. The train track travelled by Sam traversed vast moors, as well as country estates where the very rich lived – there was room unlimited. He did not get involved, however, and after a third pint walked back to his hotel.

After a hearty breakfast, Sam paid his bill and ventured on to the busy streets of the capital. According to the written instructions from Sir Harry Trafford, he was to report to a person at an address in Mayfair where he would be given details of what was expected of him.

It was a lovely morning and Sam was soon fascinated in the business of the capital. There were men in top or bowler hats carrying rolled-up umbrellas, although the chance of rain was practically nil, and women in full dresses and tight bodices wearing bonnets and long gloves despite the sun. He even passed an organ grinder, complete with a monkey in yellow trousers and a bright red jacket that had been taught to dip its cap into the nearby horse trough and drink from it; there we vendors shouting their wares, policemen giving directions, buses with open stairs at the rear, private cars, horses and carts and many black taxis.

Despite the sunlit joys all round him, Sam abandoned his written instructions about which buses to take, and headed for the Underground at King's Cross. He had only travelled on it once before, and been fascinated. At the mainline station, though, he noticed a family who seemed to be in distress. A mother wrapped in a black shawl held a baby, while two older children of about six and seven desperately held on to her skirt. At the father's feet were a wicker basket and a battered suitcase, and they all looked tired and hungry.

But the mother in particular seemed very weary, and Sam felt ashamed at noticing how beautiful she was, reminding him of an old religious painting he had seen once. He was then embarrassed because she caught his eye, and he realised she must have seen him looking at her. Then she made a gesture, as if she was asking him for help, and Sam found he could not walk away.

He realised the man – who had no English – was struggling to understand the station map, and was pointing at somewhere in the East End of the city. Realising what was needed, Sam led them over to the ticket counter. As the man searched desperately for enough money, and the woman tried to hide her growing distress, Sam pressed a banknote into his hand, and tickets to Aldgate were bought. It was far too much, but Sam refused to take the change, and they showed him passports and photographs of what must be their relatives. On another piece of paper, Aldgate station had been ringed with pencil and 3pm written next to it; it appeared they would be met there and all would be well.

At the last minute, the woman gave him another note. It was their intended East End address and she indicated that if the family was contacted there, Sam's money would be returned. He smiled and gestured that it was not necessary but she insisted he should keep the address.

Sam was further embarrassed when she kissed him on the cheek, but impulsively opened his suitcase and gave them the food his mother had packed for him. She could not hold back tears now, and everyone including the children hugged him. But they're just frightened people lost in a foreign land, he told himself, and wondered what could possibly have caused them to flee so far from home.

He also admitted to himself a tiny twinge of guilt. If his eyes hadn't lingered because the woman was so beautiful he would have passed them by. Who knew what might have happened to them then? When the train doors closed the last thing he saw was her looking back at him. He touched his cheek where she had kissed him and another wave of guilt washed over him. He picked up his suitcase, lighter now, and made his way to his own platform.

Soon – a train man through and through – Sam was lost in appreciation of the engineering marvel of the system, how cleanly, fast and smooth the carriages passed through the Tube. He wondered why they moved only on a single track in one direction, until he realised that every train pushed a mass of air in front of it. If one came from the opposite direction the pressure wave might cause problems like the water scoop under an A4 Pacific which he'd spent so much effort solving; he must discuss it with Sir Nigel Gresley!

He spent happy minutes trying to calculate what mass of air every underground engine pushed forward, and considered the benefits of running in a partial, or better still, a total vacuum. Transportation with no wind resistance: fantastic if that might be possible. When he realised he'd reached Green Park, he had to dash for the doors before he missed his stop.

Rising up on the endless loop of the wooden escalator, Sam walked out of the station back into the sunshine. He set off walking, as instructed, with Green Park on his left until he came to Bolton Street, amused at the thought of having a road in the capital named after him. His instructions led him to a grand old building in Curzon Street, and he pressed a bell under a polished brass plate indicating it was a section of the Ministry of Transport. Sam smiled to himself at his uncontrollable feeling of self-importance. What would his mates back home think if they knew what he was up to?

The impressive wooden door slowly opened, and a youth in a uniform like a telegram boy's led Sam up a staircase to a corridor that looked a modern makeshift addition to the building, where small cubicles housed individual clerks. The uniformed boy stopped outside one of them and tapped on the door. Sam was ushered in to find a man of his own age or younger standing behind a desk. Taking an offered cigarette to be polite, he was given a light from a Dunhill desktop.

After the man introduced himself as Norman Rigby and they had exchanged pleasantries, they got down to business.

'I believe Sir Harry has already briefed you about

the task ahead," said Norman. "It was a very brief brief, so to speak, because it's more or less up to you what you consider important when you arrive in Berlin. We'd like you to find out as much as you can about the Nazi's use of trains to transport troops and armaments, and if they are actually arming rolling stock."

"You mean fixing guns to carriages?"

"Yes, that sort of thing. And whether stations are being made more secure, with deep shelters or fortified structures. In short, anything that persuades you they're preparing for a war."

"But, well, I'm a draughtsman in a drawing office. Suppose I get things wrong?" Sam's self-confidence was ebbing.

Norman laughed. "Up until three months ago, I was studying languages at Cambridge. I'm only here because Uncle Harry asked me to give a hand. Don't worry about getting things wrong. Just ride about and enjoy yourself. Report back anything you think relevant to your handler, Vernon Stainton."

"My handler?"

"That's what these people call themselves. Think of him as your drawing office manager if it helps."

Sam was amused at the thought. His staid and timid manager in Doncaster running a Berlin bar!

"And I'm to stay with Vernon Stainton?"

"That's your base, but feel free to roam about

as much as you think necessary. We've made suggestions of routes you might take." Norman handed him an envelope. "Don't worry about it now, though, you'll have plenty of time to study it on the boat tonight. You land in Zeebrugge, and travel by train to Berlin. Which is when it all begins."

"Zeebrugge?"

"A port in Belgium. Quite a stretch to Berlin, I'm afraid – morning until night on the train, you'll get a chance to enjoy the scenery. You can even start making notes and taking the odd snap on your way."

"But I haven't brought a camera. I never thought to borrow one."

"We'll sort all that out later. So, don't lose that or you won't know where to go." Sam put the envelope in his inner jacket pocket and fastened the button.

"Stainton will issue you with funds at his discretion, because ultimately he'll have to sign off your expenses and justify them to this department. But don't worry about that, just keep a record of everything you spend."

"A record?" Sam looked concerned.

"Nothing too elaborate. Just keep all receipts and ticket stubs. Meals, drinks, trips to the theatre or cinema. No matter how low the value, you must keep everything and submit them to Stainton. He'll vouch for you as a temporarily employed barman."

"But I've no experience of bar work!"

"Oh, it's very simple," Norman reassured him. "I've done it myself in Cambridge. Great fun. Now, there are a few things I need to tick off. Let's whip through this list and have a bite to eat at the club. Plenty of time to get you on the boat train."

"Where do I get that?"

"Harwich. I'm going to drive you there myself. My parents live in Frinton so I'll drop you off and spend the night with them before setting off back here in the morning."

Sam was relieved, but rather underwhelmed by how casual Norman was.

"I'll take us to the club after here, and with a bit of luck we can have you delivered to Berlin before Thursday night."

"The club?" He was in London, but his thoughts dashed back to the Railwaymen's at home.

"The Savile, Brook Street. We might even squeeze in a game of snooker. Do you play?"

"Yes."

"Good. Just a few questions before we go, though." Norman produced a sheet of paper from his desk drawer. "Have you ever fired a revolver, rifle or shotgun?"

Sam thought for a few moments.

"I shot a small-calibre rifle at a row of moving

ducks at a Mayday fairground not long ago." He sounded pleased. "I knocked down seven or eight out of ten. I think that's about it."

"I think we'll just put down a no for that," said Norman. "This is a standard form to be filled in and you won't be involved with guns in any case. It would complicate things if I had to go into details involving plaster ducks – just don't pull any triggers, okay? Even under the most extreme of circumstances, leave it to the people who've been trained. Next thing's interrogation. If you're stopped and questioned about your business in Germany tell them as close to the truth as you can get."

"What, that I'm spying on the German railway system?" Norman laughed.

"Don't mention spying under any circumstances! You are what you are – a draughtsman employed by the LNER, observing the efficiency of the German railways as part of your on-going training. One day you hope to be … What? What do you hope to be?"

"A senior draughtsman. To be honest I'd really like to be a design engineer like Sir Nigel Gresley, but that's a very remote possibility."

"But an excellent answer. You're doing something to further your career. You're an admirer of the achievements of German locomotive engineers and have saved up some money to enjoy an extended leave. And you're hoping to meet some beautiful young frauleins."

"Am I?"

"Why not? A good well-rounded character. And tell them Vernon Stainton's a distant relative, which explains why you're staying with him. Right, that's almost everything. On our way to lunch we'll stop off down the corridor and pick up your passport. You did bring a photograph with you as we asked?"

"Yes, from the family album."

"Splendid."

Sam handed the photograph to Norman, who was satisfied it filled the bill.

"It's from my sister Gwen's recent wedding."

"Very good. That's almost everything then. The man who has your passport will loan you a simple camera and some rolls of film. Return both and he'll develop them. Snap anything that looks of interest, and don't forget the usual tourist attractions."

"All right. I hope it isn't an expensive model. But I will look after it."

"I'm sure you will. And so, to lunch," said Norman. Then he announced, with some satisfaction: "Samuel Bolton of Doncaster, under the wing of distant relative Vernon Stainton. Travelling hither and thither observing the German railway system to further his career. Perfect. Oh, another thing. When away staying in hotels or guest houses don't avoid other travellers and guests. Engage them in conversation when it seems natural, and be open about your reason to be wherever you are. You are a railwayman, a keen and dedicated employee of Sir Nigel Gresley, whom you wish to emulate. Agreed?"

"Agreed." Sam said. And they stepped out towards the door.

As promised, Sam was given his passport, a wad of German marks worth twenty pounds sterling, and the camera and films. He signed for everything and then noticed the boat ticket was to the Hook of Holland, not Zeebrugge, which Norman dismissed as a detail, saying there was not much difference. Sam found this a shade disquieting. He hoped Vernon Stainton in Berlin would be more efficient at passing on the experience and expertise that might be needed.

He was encouraged by the prospect of a game of snooker, a ride in the country and a boat to Holland, though, all of which made him feel as if he was going on an exciting holiday. The fact that it was all paid for by somebody else was even better.

The Savile Club in Mayfair was another revelation. There was an impressive sweeping staircase ahead and to the left, while on his right stood a man in a smart uniform who was undoubtedly an ex-soldier. Norman vouched for his guest and they walked into a bar area with a high ceiling, wood-panelled walls and an oriental-patterned carpet. Sam's mind was boggling. He had imagined that the Savile would possibly be in the same kind of bracket as Doncaster Railwaymen's Club.

They were literally worlds apart.

SEVEN

Vernon Stainton had been in charge of the Berlin business for almost seven years, in which time it had suffered a modest decline. He was a lazy and neglectful landlord, but the passing trade refused to let the bar become unprofitable, and it supported him and half a dozen staff. When he looked back on his life – as he did frequently after brandy – he had to smile at his luck. He'd been born an only child into a family with a tradition of public service, with his mother a secretary to a Member of Parliament and his father a middle-ranking civil servant. After minor public school, he'd scraped through university to an almost obligatory career in his father's footsteps.

His name and family reputation helped him survive various mishaps, until he made the debutante daughter of a minor aristocrat pregnant. The scandal was hushed up, and Vernon was shipped out to the British Embassy in Berlin. He was no diplomat but soon became aware of his worth. Not only had he tainted a noble family but also, he discovered, had shared a mistress with the future King of England. Whispered conversations in corridors of power resulted in him being kept abroad, and a new post quickly found for him. Vernon Stainton was to take over the bar in Berlin, paid for by the British Government, until something even farther from England and harm could be organised.

Sadly, the baby had died, and with the abdication of Edward VIII in 1936 Vernon's stock had plummeted. He managed to cling on largely unnoticed in his backwater, with the salary of a low-grade civil servant and the bar takings thrown in, but his main source of income was selling British passports to people in dire need of escape from Germany. The Secret Service turned a blind eye in the main, but it gave them a useful hold on him – such as providing lodgings to the 'trainspotter'. Vernon knew he had to keep London sweet, and in particular Sir Harry Trafford, his new boss.

Sam found it strange to be eating fish on a Wednesday, especially in the spacious dining room where portraits of past members looked down upon them. However, he found it very enjoyable and afterwards was shown into the snooker room, which was astonishing. He enjoyed playing the game back home, but the railwaymen's social club had once been part of a shunting shed; hardly the splendour of a Mayfair Gentleman's Club.

He and Norman played several games, with Sam forbidden, as a non-member, from buying drinks or even paying for his share of lunch. It was honours even when time called a halt to their close-fought frames, but they were determined to play again on Sam's return. They liked each other's company.

The journey to Harwich was no less enjoyable in Norman's open-topped car in the early summer sunshine. It was an MGA VA Tourer and everything about it sparkled: the wire wheels, deep red almost purple body, with large shiny headlights and a single spot between. They sped along in light tan leather seats chatting like old friends.

"I could never imagine being away at school," Sam said after Norman had explained his family circumstances. He had been a boarder fifty miles from home.

"I never considered it odd. My brother had been there before me, and it was the normal course of things. So, you didn't go to university?"

"No," Sam said. It had never even been a possibility. "When I left school my dad had been working overtime and saving so I could become an apprentice at The Plant."

"What's the plant?" Norman asked, accelerating down a long straight stretch of road, to their delight.

"The London and North Eastern Railway's Locomotive Works at Doncaster," Sam shouted above the roar of the engine.

"You seem to take great pride in saying that,"

Norman said, without edge.

"I do. It's a great place to work. I'm a railwayman from a railway family. How good is that?"

They both laughed at the simplicity of the statement and their shared enjoyment of travelling in an open-topped car in the sunshine. When Norman had to slow down behind a tractor and the engine noise was quieter, Sam asked about his own circumstances.

"I want to travel and put some of my linguistic skills to the test," he said. "But if we do go to war, all our plans will fly out of the window, won't they? Will you join up?"

"I expect I'll have to," Sam replied. Although to be honest, he had never given it much serious thought.

"You may be in a reserved occupation."

"I don't know. I'll do whatever's right I suppose. If it comes to it, will you be an officer, Norman?"

"I expect so. My father was in the last big bash, and both my brother and I were officers in the cadets at school."

"At school?" Sam asked incredulously.

"Yes. Didn't you have any military training at yours?"

"No. But I was captain of the football and rugby teams if that counts!"

"It might get you to be a lance-corporal," Norman

joked back, and they both laughed.

By the time they parted at the port of Harwich, Norman had given Sam his office and home telephone numbers, and recapped all the vital points made earlier. Sam disembarked at dawn, and walked to the Hoek van Holland railway station, which was adjacent. By trial and error he managed to buy a ticket for Berlin and find the correct platform.

The train, which arrived soon after, was pulled by a huge steam locomotive built by Beyer Peacock in Manchester, which amused Sam: so, no German diesels here then! He climbed aboard and settled in an empty carriage to catch up on his sleep. Securing his suitcase in a rack above his head, he jammed himself into a seat and closed his eyes – to be awoken almost two hours later to find six people crammed into the carriage giving him accusing looks. His blustered apology for taking up two places was well received, to his relief, and his fellow travellers seemed amused. He was an embarrassed Englishman. The ice was broken.

Sam was surprised to find so many English speakers in the carriage, and keen to practice their language skills on him. He was bombarded with questions about himself and his country, and the atmosphere was very friendly – some sharing food and drink so that he did not go hungry.

Bruno and Max, the Schafer twins, had always been reluctant farmers. They had become more and more obsessed with joining the army with every speech heard on the wireless in the bedroom they shared with two of their brothers, absorbing every morsel of propaganda put out by the National Socialists. They believed, without question, everything Hitler and his supporters said.

Moving to Berlin had been their long-standing ambition, and they had arrived two months earlier, in time for Hitler's 49th birthday celebrations, to share a dingy low-rent flat.

Everything about the city overwhelmed them. Each government building, and many private businesses, had been draped in the stark red and black swastika emblem flags, and the birthday was the night of their lives. On the unfamiliar wide streets, grinning inanely, they were hugged by strangers as hysteria swept through the city.

"He is coming, he is coming," was the cry from the crowds. Some wept and others laughed uncontrollably in anticipation at seeing the only person to matter in their lives, the Führer – believed by some to be as close to the second coming of Christ as the world would ever witness. Max and Bruno felt so ecstatic, so privileged to be where they were.

Young, fit and desperate to dedicate themselves to *him* and their country, they would join the army at the earliest possibility and they would serve with every fibre of their beings.

Unfortunately, so far, they had met obstructions to their ambitions. The army had not welcomed them as warmly as they had anticipated, and instead had put them on a reserve list, with the reason cited 'low intelligence'.

Even this, however, did not shake their faith. As they had grown up practically uneducated on the family farm, it seemed unsurprising that they'd been considered almost idiots. And they would right this misunderstanding! They would improve themselves! Obtaining a copy of the speech Joseph Goebbels had given for Hitler's birthday celebrations, they learned some passages by heart, and quoted them to each other as a demonstration of their growing education. They would achieve!

Their belief in Hitler was blind and absolute; they accepted without question he was the future of Germany, the unique way forward. He would keep them safe from all harm in a rebuilt land that would last a thousand years. He had provided work and bread for all the people, and from that came pride and self-respect. There was work for everyone, as there should be, without shirkers or cheats.

Bruno and Max reasoned that they would prove

themselves through their newfound education. In addition, they would demonstrate that they already had the basic skills required by the army: they could kill without hesitation.

They had grown up slaughtering all forms of animals, including rats, and a propaganda film they saw one night likened rats, explicitly, to Jews. They knew then that they had a role to play in helping Hitler build the Fatherland.

Max and Bruno would prove their worth by exterminating Jews. They would kill again that very evening before reporting to their contact in the bar.

They would succeed and impress.

After crossing into Germany, almost all the passengers said "Heil Hitler" on arriving and departing, and everyone else replied in unison. At first Sam did not participate, thinking it was not his place, until an old man sitting opposite encouraged him to join in the salute.

He seemed unnecessarily sombre. He fixed him with a steady gaze and said quietly:

"If Heil Hitler is said to you, always say it back. Always."

Sam complied. What harm could be in that?

His first experience of the German railway system was that it was fast, clean and pleasant. They passed through quaint villages of half-timbered houses with flowering window boxes and lush gardens, reminiscent in many ways of rural England. Although being hauled by steam today, and not naturally disposed to diesel engines, he accepted that statistics proved they were becoming more and more efficient with each generation the Germans developed.

England, however, had an unlimited supply of coal, while he wasn't sure about Germany's access to crude oil to refine as diesel fuel. Whatever the cold facts in any case, with engineers like Sir Nigel Gresley, the likes of the A4 Pacific class would continue to run the length and breadth of Britain for a long time to come.

Sam did concede a diesel locomotive, the *Fliegender Hamburger*, held the world speed record, but he also knew Sir Nigel was determined to design and run faster engines. He had upgraded his already successful A3 Pacific to make the new generation of A4s, and it would not be long before the title was in Britain, where it belonged.

Sir Nigel had been convinced of the importance of streamlining since the early '30s, and the elegant covering on the A4 was inspired by a Bugatti rail-car he had seen in France. Other changes from the A3 included an increase in boiler pressure, and smaller cylinders with bigger valves.

Sam himself had worked on modifications

including the Kylchap double-blastpipe exhaust and Westinghouse brake valves, and he was anxious – determined even – to be home in England for the final trials.

Rumours in The Plant were rife. Sir Nigel – HNG as he was known to all – was planning an attempt for the very near future. Speculation that 110mph might be reached was excitedly discussed, although Sir Nigel himself refused to name a number, or a date. But everyone was mightily encouraged by his air of quiet confidence.

Bruno and Max looked down at the body with professional satisfaction. It had been a clean kill without unnecessary suffering, though that was not their priority. When the time came to show off their skills they would be more than happy to prolong an execution. They would also torture, if asked to do so, to extract information or for any other reason. They had once tortured a dog that would not submit to their will and training. They had taken it out of earshot of the farmhouse because it would perversely perform tricks for a sister who was fond of it. They killed it over two full hours, impressed at its stubbornness and will to live. Ultimately the brothers had domineered. They had destroyed the worthless creature.

"How many more?" Max asked.

"Until …" said Bruno, with an enigmatic smile.

Max needed more.

"… until people start asking 'who could be killing these Jews in such an efficient way?'" Bruno said. "Asking 'who are these people clearing the streets of vermin without making themselves known or seeking a reward?' Until enough people start to say 'We want to meet and thank them for cleansing without prompting. We, the people, will override the petty laws that still exist to stop such noble actions. We, the people, want Bruno and Max to join our glorious army and lead other men into action against the rabid Jew.' When the time is right, brother, we will show ourselves, and be honoured."

Max had noticed that Bruno had developed a strut of late, a way of talking quite different from when they had been back home in the country. It made him wary and subservient. His unpredictable brother had a dangerous temperament.

"So, she is not the last?" he asked.

"No," said Bruno. "Haven't you been listening to me? We must prove ourselves, but also make contacts like the man in the bar. He served in the last war, works for the party and eventually will be called up from reserve. We'll continue helping him collect his debts. He rewards us well, and when the time is right we'll tell him of our other deeds and pledge our loyalty. Agreed?"

Max nodded. "Agreed, my brother."

EIGHT

Herta was dressed in her usual working clothes of black tight skirt and billowing white blouse, showing much cleavage as she leaned on the business side of the bar smiling at Willy, her most regular customer, who was seated on a barstool. Vernon was reading the latest telegram from London. Herta had decoded it and was waiting for her tutor's first impression: 'New barman. Mad keen trainspotter arriving imminently. Family delighted you will accommodate'

It was signed Uncle Harry, Vernon's new boss, and he feared Sir Harry Trafford was as keen to find out about himself as he was about the German railway system. Vernon knew he was under scrutiny. So the guest would be arriving very soon. He had to send a good impression back.

Sam arrived at Potsdamer Bahnhof in good spirits. He walked slowly up the busy platform taking in his new surroundings. It was a very busy station filled mainly with Berliners going briskly about their business, and the usual farewells of parting couples and families. He also saw the occasional sights of lost souls and families as he had witnessed at King's Cross. But he was in a foreign land. He must not concern himself with such matters.

The overwhelming feeling was that of thriving industrious people happy to go about their business. A small brass band was playing outside a café and some people were even dancing. It was a sight that made him stop and smile, as he could not imagine such spontaneity in Doncaster. He decided to linger and have a coffee as many trains came and went. Sam had no idea of most of the destinations, although he could decipher that the train was headed for a major city like Paris or Cologne. A man at the next table, proud to be able to speak English, was happy to engage him in conversation.

"Your famous countryman, Robert Stephenson, is honoured here," he said, annunciating proudly to perfection. "His locomotive *Adler* – which means the Eagle – was the very first train to arrive one hundred years ago, at this very station. There is a replica down the platform which you must see. I will take you."

On their brief trip, Sam told his companion almost the full truth of his reason to be in Berlin, but after he had gone Sam vowed to himself not to be so ready with explanations any more. The people he'd encountered had been so friendly it was difficult not to open up to them, and by the time he'd seen the replica of Stephenson's *Adler*, he was convinced the only difference between the two countries was the language. He just could not envisage another war between them.

"I have every word correct?" Herta asked, returning to the bar after serving customers.

"Yes," said Vernon shortly. News of the imminent arrival had unnerved him. It would upset his lax routine.

"And I know what every word means," Herta added proudly. "My English is bloody good."

"Yes, very good. But I can't have our guest thinking I allow just anyone to have knowledge of my communications."

The regular, Willy Diefenbaker, held out his empty glass.

"But that's part of the fun of coming in here, Vernon," he said. He was wearing a smart suit and top coat, despite the warm weather. He felt it appropriate for an accountant and minor National Socialist Party officer.

Herta took the glass and began refilling it.

"Do I stay or go during his visit?" she pouted. She was hardly just a maid, was she? "Of course you stay. His arrival doesn't turn me into a bloody monk. What a stupid question."

"Well since you found out about him you have been even more grumpy than usual, so I thought I'd better ask. Do you agree, Willy?"

"Oh, don't drag me into your domestic quarrel.

Do you think he's here to spy on you as well as our railways Vernon?"

"I can't be too bloody careful. If this man's tight with my new boss Trafford I could be facing close scrutiny myself."

"Not worried about the sack are you, Vernon?" Willy asked with some concern.

"I need to be careful. I might be looking to send a snippet or two back home, just for insurance purposes."

"What sort of things?"

"Reports of promotions within the party machine, maybe. Berlin installing air raid sirens, that sort of thing."

"I'll see what I can do." Willy said, now also worried that the arrival of the new man could upset the apple cart.

"And I'll put it into code," Herta said playfully, knowing it would exasperate Vernon.

"You won't go anywhere near that codebook or my telegrams for the foreseeable future. Is that clear, Herta? This is serious stuff."

"And our business?" asked Willy seriously.

"Will of course go on. We just don't want anybody rocking the boat. Especially as the prices are going up and up."

Willy agreed with a solemn nod of his head. The "business" involved Vernon and himself supplying

British passports and German travel documents to needy escapees for a very high price. Ostensibly, they were part of an escape route for people in danger of a regime that was becoming increasingly totalitarian and intolerant, but in reality the two men had no interest in protecting the vulnerable and the poor – they sold the papers to those who could afford to pay. As the desperation grew, the cost increased accordingly. Vernon and Willy were making a lot of money from their cruel trade.

Willy was thinking.

"This man coming to spy on our trains. Is that because your people have designs on taking away our world speed record?"

"I neither know nor care," said Vernon, topping up his brandy glass. "And neither should you."

Willy became straighter and taller with nationalistic pride.

"You may be uninterested in national records," he said stiffly, "but I'm immensely proud of our achievements under the leadership of the Führer."

He looked to Herta for support. Herta just shrugged.

"Willy, keep the bloody world record, I really don't care," said Vernon, with a dismissive gesture. "I don't want my world interfered with, that's all."

Willy would not let it go.

"But if that is the purpose of your trainspotter

guest, I have to say I will not like it."

"Bloody hell, Willy! It's prep school antics. You and me are realists, right?"

Willy bristled. He regarded Vernon as an amusing friend, but also a louche character who had an attitude not befitting a companion of one following the guidance of the Führer. But he was also fond of the easy money they were making.

Vernon also needed Willy, and thought it best to mollify him.

"Willy, you are a serious member of your party and I respect that," he said. "I support the King of England and all that he stands for, and I've even shared female friends with his brother – but that's another story. Suffice to say we're both patriotic in our own ways. But the bottom line is, we have to look after ourselves. Agreed?"

"What are you getting at, Vernon? You think I should keep quiet about our speed record?"

"I'm not saying that. Let's just give this trainspotter and my bosses back in London what they want. He'll soon be on his way, but he comes here expecting a loyal, faithful servant of the realm and we shouldn't shatter that illusion. By all means speak up for your beliefs and speed records, but remember that as far as you know I'm just an English landlord. Not a spy."

"All right, I will pretend I don't know what you

really are."

"Can I pretend you're the best lover in Berlin?" Herta asked.

"You can go and collect the glasses from outside," Vernon snapped. As she left, he said to Willy, "and as business is going to continue, although maybe a little lower key than usual, let me ask about our most outstanding debt."

"It will be taken care of," Willy said. "I've told him once a passport is ordered it must be paid for, and his mother dying is his problem, not ours. The passport's ready and the payment should be the same. He may be thinking of reneging on our agreement, who knows? But the boys are paying him a visit."

Vernon winced. "Does that have to happen? They frighten the life out of me." Willy laughed. "That's the whole point, my friend. Our debt will be recovered. No question about that."

The middle-aged man had no way of beating the two collectors standing in his dining-room. He was in mourning for his mother, but his overwhelming emotion was fear. He looked into the dead eyes of Bruno and Max, and saw little recognisably human.

"You can see for yourselves how she lies in peace." The open coffin was supported by two substantial dining chairs. "I bury her tomorrow, and she doesn't need a passport to get to heaven. Suppose I pay you half? I think that's a fair resolution to our situation."

Bruno and Max's only response was a shared look. Without word or hesitation they gripped the side of the coffin and spilled the dead woman on to the floor. Her son screamed his disbelief and horror, then froze in terror as the corpse was stamped on by the twins.

"Stop, stop, stop!" he shouted as he tried to put himself between the attackers and their dead victim. But they swatted him away.

"I'll pay you. Please stop. I will give you all the money."

"Do we kill him?" Max asked, earnestly.

"No. He's not a Jew." Bruno thought it best to check. "Are you a Jew?"

"No, no, no," the man answered, as he fumbled to count out what he owed. He was disinclined to tell them that his sexual orientation was his need to flee the country.

Sam was travelling by taxi to Vernon's bar on the Kurfürstendamm. Everywhere seemed so clean in the sunshine, with huge black and red flags flying from many buildings, and everyone so smartly dressed. He was impressed by how modern Berlin was – almost futuristic compared with drab Doncaster, Leeds or Sheffield. Even London with all its magnificent buildings seemed very staid and dated to him now. Berlin was the future.

NINE

Erna's fiancé Ralf was a slight, nervous young man at the best of times, but now he could hardly control his shaking body. He had not slept since he had realised Erna had gone missing, torn between staying in his lodgings waiting for her to arrive or walking the streets in search of her. He had been in a state of ecstasy when he found they'd obtained the necessary papers, and had said the words over and over to himself, "The United States of America." A new life, where he and Erna could work, prosper and raise a family. The land of the free.

That unbridled joy and hope now seemed ridiculous. It was as if he had exceeded the quota of happiness allowed to him by fate. He should have known that it was never meant to be and he was now paying the price for such presumption. When he arrived at the Rossenhoff's, he was in as much despair as he had been happy. Helena hurried him inside.

"Have you had any word?" she asked. "Anything at all?"

Ralf shook his head. Even though he had not, he had an overwhelming feeling of grief that Erna was either dead or in a desperate situation. He could think of no reason why she had not met him as planned the day she left the Rosenhoff's house. She had so looked forward to her new life and he knew only an extreme diversion would have stopped them being together. He also knew that in the climate that pervaded Berlin for people such as they, anything was possible. Their rights had been so eroded that bullies, conmen and thieves saw them as natural victims and preyed on them with growing immunity. He was sick with trepidation.

Helena brought tea into the lounge where Ralf was sitting with her father.

"The police were so dismissive. As if she did not matter," he was saying. "I felt so ineffective, because it's true. I did not matter either. None of us do in their eyes. She could be anywhere."

Jacob Rosenhoff looked pitifully at the young desperate man. He needed to offer hope.

"No news is … something." he said, and felt immediately helpless and stupid having uttered such a platitude.

"Can you think of anything she might have said as she was leaving?" Ralf asked, not for the first time.

"We have thought and thought of anything she said that might help. Thought and thought.

But … no." said Jacob.

They had exhausted all their lines of local enquiry. Neighbours had been questioned, the police contacted, and they had walked the streets in the vain hope of finding out what might have happened to the young woman they all loved. But it was as if she had never existed. Her twenty years of life had made no impact except to those three who had known her so well and seen her grow and flourish.

After a while there had been little more to say or do, so Ralf had left them on the doorstep promising to inform them of any news. The promise was reciprocated and they had separated – none the wiser or more reassured than when they had met an hour earlier.

Sam paid for the taxi, obtained a receipt as drummed into him by Norman, thanked the driver and stood with his suitcase outside the bar. He could not have felt happier. Three young women were sitting at an outside table enjoying lunch in the sunshine, pretty and radiating happiness, and Sam boldly nodded a greeting before stepping inside. Despite Vernon being a lazy landlord, first impressions were of sparkling cleanliness, because the bar was tiled and kept clean by two women who arrived every morning to rid the place of debris from the night before. Vernon paid them well and never interfered with their routine. Sometimes he did not see them from payday to payday. It was a good, simple relationship.

Ornate tiles depicting an action scene adorned one wall. It was of dogs attacking a deer while huntsmen ran after them. A large mirror was behind the bar, reflecting optics and bottles on gleaming glass shelves. Bar stools lined up against the sturdy mahogany counter, and wooden tables and chairs filled the rest of the space, spilling into the street from opening to closing time. Vernon encouraged some regular customers to bring them indoors with the offer of the last drink. They always obliged, saving him the effort.

Herta saw Sam first, rightly assuming he was the expected guest by his English clothes, more fit for winter than summer, and his very old suitcase. Her first impression was of some handsome young man whose naïve appraisal of the bar shouted out 'tourist', with an aura of athleticism and boyish charm. She thought she might like him, but treated him as any other patron rather than the expected trainspotter. She left it to him to introduce himself.

"Hello, I'm sorry but I am English and my German is non-existent."

"My English is bloody good." Herta said smiling and very proud of herself. "Terrific!" Sam said. "I am looking for another Englishman, Vernon Stainton. He's a distant relative of mine and has offered to put me up for a while. I'm here on holiday."

"You are the trainspotter," she said knowingly, putting him on the wrong foot.

"Er … well, yes, I suppose I am," he said, hoping

no one was in earshot.

"He's upstairs resting. I will go and tell him you are here. Sit down and have a drink while you are waiting." She called another barmaid and disappeared upstairs.

Erna's body was discovered by children playing hide and seek. Two nine-year old girls had hidden near a playground close to the building where they lived and had come across the gruesome sight. Erna's neck had been broken, and she lay like a discarded damaged mannequin under her winter coat. Jet-black hair covered half her face, and what was visible was white with a blueish hue around her lips. The open staring eyes emphasised the transformation from a lively young woman to a lifeless dummy.

The little girls stared in fascination. And wondered why a note was attached to the lapel of the coat. It read 'JUDE'.

At first, the adults thought that it was part of the girls' fantasy – an extension of their hiding game from their other friend, who now felt left out of the thrill of the discovery. But her parents thanked God that she'd been spared the trauma of seeing the pitiful body: they had Jewish ancestry, and anything that drew the attention of the authorities might be dangerous.

The police went through the motions of

investigating the violent crime, but had little incentive to pursue it. Her appearance, the quality of her clothes, her meagre possessions meant she was of little value. Erna was a Jew and her body had been despatched to the morgue. Her papers showed the Rosenhoff's address as her dwelling and detectives would visit them.

"He's sorry to keep you waiting but he won't be too long. Official business," Herta said pleasantly as she rejoined Sam in the bar.

"I understand," Sam replied returning her smile and discreetly keeping his eyes away from her ample bosom.

"I am Herta," she said, holding out her hand and smiling.

"Sam. Sam Bolton." He guessed she was mid to late thirties. She was slightly chubby and quite attractive, and he imagined his mother would describe her as a country girl with rosy cheeks and a good complexion, while sisters Gwen and Edith would probably call her 'brassy'.

Sam, though, assumed she was not dressed unusually for a barmaid in a warm city. His experience of bar staff back at home was largely limited to his dour Doncaster Railway Men's Club, where an old fireman ran things at his own pace and service was shunting speed rather than express. He also occasionally drank in a pub near the cinema and enjoyed waitress service from an arthritic woman who was in her sixties at least.

Slightly embarrassed lest Herta guessed his thoughts, Sam told her he would wait for Vernon in the afternoon sunshine. He took his drink and case outside, hoping to see the three fraüleins again, but they had finished lunch and gone, so he sat at their vacated table. The audible chatter from people passing by reminded him that he was far from home, which he found exciting; the impenetrable language only added to the adventure. He knew he would have no chance of being mistaken for a native, and would heed the advice given to just be a tourist who was keen on trains.

He sipped the beer cautiously, being immediately and pleasantly surprised by the taste. It was nothing like he had experienced before; it was cold and very palatable. Sam thought of home and what Edgar would say if he knew his brother-in-law was sitting in the sunshine with a very good beer, and being paid to drink it. This made him even happier.

After a little while, Vernon stepped from the bar carrying a cup of tea. It wouldn't take him long to assess the visitor's status and threat to his own well-being, and he genuinely believed that there wouldn't be war between England and his adopted country. In such times of uncertainty, however, he was ideally placed to amass a small fortune exploiting Jews who wanted to escape Berlin. After they'd been purged, and Germany had regained the territory that she had every right to, everything would settle down again, and he could continue to enjoy his dissipated lifestyle in better times. Sam Bolton's visit should only be a blip in his long-term plan; and one easily dealt with.

Vernon studied the young man sitting in the sunshine, guessing he was dressed in his Sunday best for the journey: an inexpensive dark suit complete with waistcoat and fob watch. To Vernon's relief he was definitely working class, and probably not well travelled, looking far too interested in his surroundings to be anything but a tourist, an image boosted by the fact he had a suitcase at his feet and had not had the sense to leave it behind the bar. He clearly had an eye for passing girls though – which was good – but after checking the contents of his wallet left it on the table, which was trusting and stupid. An inexperienced young man, then, who could be easily handled by the far more life-qualified ex-public schoolboy.

He stepped out to where Sam would see him, older, urbane, relaxed, and instinctively Sam knew he was his host, so rose to his feet. Vernon anticipated his greeting.

"Sam Bolton, I presume," he said, and the two Englishmen exchanged greetings. Vernon then gestured for Sam to sit back down and welcomed him to his home. After small talk about Sam's recruitment to the service and journey to Berlin they felt relaxed in each other's company and Vernon was happily in charge.

"You've arrived here at a momentous time in Germany's history," he said. "It's an era of great optimism and patriotism. Hitler has them all fired up and looking forward to the future."

"You enjoy being here, then?" Sam replied, and his lack of an insightful question gave Vernon confidence that all would go well with the visit.

"I do." Vernon paused to convey gravitas before he spoke again. "But I never forget that I'm here to do a good job for my country. I may appear to be very easy going sometimes, and some might say not too serious, but don't be fooled. I've made many friends in important places by playing a frivolous ex-patriot unconcerned with politics."

He laughed lightly.

"You'll see what I mean as time goes on. Just do as I say and everything will be fine. The last thing I need is some hot-head messing things up for me. Understand?"

"Absolutely," Sam said, earnestly. He was not sure how business like this was normally conducted, so he added: "I'm a pure amateur at what I've been asked to do here, so I'll be taking your lead. You do … you do know why I'm here, don't you?"

"Of course I do, young man! As senior operative in Berlin I've been informed fully of your mission, and you'll be reporting everything to me – everything. You do understand that, don't you?"

"Yes, sir," Sam replied. He was afraid that Vernon might have taken offence. Which Vernon played on.

"Then just to make sure you know exactly what's expected," he said, gravely, "tell me what you consider your mission to be here. Exactly."

Sam swallowed.

"I was asked by Sir Harry Trafford, with Sir Nigel Gresley's approval, to assess German rearming from a railway perspective," he said. "Which I take to be riding around on trains taking notes and photographs of anything I think looks like it has something military to do with the system."

He stopped, feeling rather lame.

"It all seems very casual, doesn't it?" he said. "But as far as I know, that's about it." Vernon took his time before replying. He sipped his tea and after a few minutes spoke with innate authority. Sam hung on his every word.

"Well there's no question that rearmament is taking place on a grand scale," he said, "but it's no surprise to anyone who knows this country in depth."

He looked deep into Sam's eyes.

"They suffered defeat and massive humiliation

in the war," he continued, quietly. "And then we rubbed their noses in it afterwards. Herr Hitler has given them back some self-respect, and the country's booming, and in my opinion rearmament is part of the boosting of the industrial mainstay of the nation, along with the revitalisation of the infrastructure."

Suddenly, he was more relaxed.

"The roads, the buildings, the whole bloody place is being modernised beyond anyone's wildest dreams back in Blighty," he laughed. "It's a great place to be, Sam – so you enjoy your stay. And that's an order!"

"Thank you. I'll do my best sir," Sam replied.

"Vernon. And don't expect to see me behave like a stiff-collared pen pusher from Whitehall. Understood? I've developed my own very efficient way of blending in here."

"Understood," Sam said. "Vernon …" He was wondering where Herta fitted in to the set up now. She seemed to be more than just a hired help.

"And what do you do for a living back home?" Vernon asked, fooling Sam that he really cared.

"I work in a drawing office at LNER's depot in Doncaster." Sam replied, happy to be on safe ground.

"That's Yorkshire, isn't it?"

"Yes, have you ever been there?"

"Once, I believe. A shooting weekend on some distant relative's estate. Didn't much enjoy it. I think it rained the whole time. This is the weather for me.

I hope it stays like this for the duration of your trip. Brings out the best in the fraüleins."

"Yes, I have noticed," Sam said, thinking back to his drawing office manager and how inappropriate such a comment would be to him.

"And I have no intention of being your moral guardian, Sam. There are many attractive young women in this city, and a young handsome man like you … well! I'll be obliged to write reports on your stay with me, of course, but rest assured that as long as your work is carried out conscientiously, you're free to be as libertine as you like with your time off."

Sam grinned at his new-found companion. He was going to enjoy himself …

TEN

The news spread quickly in the tightly knit community where the Rosenhoffs lived. A young woman had been found murdered in a dry ditch by a children's playground. Her killer had pinned a note to her heavy coat which labelled her a Jew. Jacob heard this in a local café where he met his friends once a week to share their troubles and their (very few) joys. From the description, he knew straight away that it was Erna, and left for home knowing the news would be devastate his daughter. He did not know if Ralf knew yet, but was sure the tragic information would destroy the young man's life. Jacob was in despair.

Erna had not even been a committed Jew, having lost any faith she might have had after her mother had died. It seemed to Jacob even more pointless and ridiculous to die because of a quirk of fate determining her religion at birth, and on his miserable walk home, he questioned, not for the first time of late, his commitment to God.

He then found himself quietly reciting a prayer for the recently deceased: "May her place of rest be in the Garden of Eden. Therefore, may the All-Merciful One shelter her with the cover of His wings forever, and bind her soul in the bond of life. The Lord is her heritage; may she rest in her resting-place in peace; and let us say: Amen." To find himself instinctively thinking these words resolved that his own bonds to Judaism were unbreakable. He also knew that his earthly mission was becoming more pressing by the hour. He must somehow find a way to attend the planned conference in Évian and highlight the plight of his people in Berlin.

Helena paled as she saw her father enter their house much earlier than was expected. His expression was enough to tell her that he was the bearer of grave news, and she sat down as he confirmed her worst fears. Then, when sufficiently composed, they decided that they must visit Ralf. He lived a short distance away by tram and Helena and her father spoke little on the journey, each reflecting that it would and should have been the first leg of Erna's passage to a better future.

They alighted at the stop, and walked a hundred yards or so to the apartment building where Ralf lived. Nearby was a post office flying a large black and red flag bearing a swastika. There was little breeze, and yet somehow it fluttered into an impressive display as they passed by, seeming to give more merit than was justified to the shabby little building. The ruling party symbol had become omnipresent in recent times, and it filled the Rosenhoffs and their compatriots with increasingly deep foreboding. The black, red and ancient symbol represented a future from which the Jewish people were to be debarred.

Helena and Jacob entered Ralf's apartment building to be stopped by a gaunt middle-aged man sitting in the entrance. He greeted them with a surly smile, raised his right arm and said, "Heil Hitler."

Being Jews they were banned from returning the salutation, and instead looked quickly from one to the other and then back at the man. They assumed him to be some sort of caretaker and he now stood and took on an arrogant posture and expression.

"Jews?" he said. Already knowing.

Jacob nodded. He was by nature an affable and confident man, but had had to learn to adopt a different manner in case his customary geniality could be taken for arrogance and used against him. "We are looking for the apartment of Ralf Meisinger," he said.

He then felt uneasy, although he did not know why. There was something about the caretaker that disturbed him; something from the past was niggling in his brain. The caretaker took his time replying. He gestured briskly to a sheet of paper on a roughly made shelf.

"Sign in and state the purpose of your visit."

Jacob picked up a pencil from the shelf and did as bid.

"337. Third floor," the caretaker told them after

checking the paper and looking disdainfully at the visitors. They headed in the direction he was indicating.

"Not so pompous now, Rosenhoff," the man said after them.

Jacob did not turn, but he could imagine the man sneering at them as they made their way to the stairs.

"What did he mean, papa?" Helena asked, as they ascended. And Jacob had remembered. Years ago, he had dismissed him and another man for misconduct in his furniture factory where they worked. They organised card games during breaks, and there was a strong suspicion they were cheating. Many men had lost significant amounts of money to the pair, and Jacob had not hesitated in giving them the sack. The dismissals had been a popular move with the remaining workers, then. Now, the sleazy conman found himself a position of petty power. A caretaker. And, no doubt, an informer for the party.

Ralf opened the door to his home, and they knew immediately he had heard the tragic news. It was as if life had been drained from him as he silently ushered them into his drab lodgings, and for the next twenty minutes, no amount for mutual consoling would come close to diminishing the grief that pervaded the room. All that could be hoped for was a decent burial for Erna, paid for by Jacob Rosenhoff, and that her murderer be brought to justice.

Ralf had been interviewed by the police and dismissed as a suspect. He had asked what would happen to her body, and been told to report to the station in two days. By that time, it was probable that a decision might have been made regarding his fiancée's remains. He was sceptical that the police would investigate the murder, or that anybody, indeed, even considered it a matter of much importance.

Sam enjoyed an extremely warm welcome at Vernon's bar. The party atmosphere was not what he'd anticipated on his first night in the German capital, assuming his appearance would be a low-key affair, with him being integrated quietly into Stainton's world. But he quickly learned that Vernon had meant what he had said. He was no stick-in-the-mud civil servant, but a man embracing his role as a fun-loving bar owner to the hilt.

The young Yorkshireman had never seen such a diverse gathering of people. Clusters of middle-aged men, couples, younger single people meeting before moving on, and exotic creatures beyond all experience. Flamboyantly dressed women who were loud, outrageous in their gestures and seemingly bigger than any he had experienced in Doncaster. It was not so much that they were fat – he knew many fat people back home – these were bigger framed and dare he think it, manly. Three of them descended on him as he was having a drink with Vernon and Herta.

"So, this is the Englishman, Vernon. How lovely. Do you know the King?" asked a heavily made-up woman. Sam's first impression was of long dark eyelashes being flapped in his face.

"Er, no," Sam faltered, as the trio gathered close to him.

"An English gentleman," a second woman said. "We are deeply honoured."

"I too am an Englishman," Vernon said flatly, but clearly not the least bit surprised by the onslaught.

"But old," said the first woman, dismissing Vernon with a gesture and concentrating intently on the Yorkshireman.

"And I knew the ex-King's ex-mistress. Knew her very well." Vernon said it matter of factly, knowing it would not impress.

"We know, we know, Vernon," the second woman said, with theatrical boredom. "You have mentioned it before. Many times before."

"Here's a young man with fresh tales to tell."

The third of the trio spoke for the first time, standing much too close to Sam for comfort.

"And doesn't he have a charming smile."

"A lovely expression," said the first. She was biting

lightly on the pearl necklace around her throat.

"That's bafflement, dear," said the second, and Sam silently agreed.

"He's choosing which one of us to like the best!"

"Choose me!"

"No, me!"

"Me!" they chorused, and Sam blushed scarlet, which made them laugh much louder.

"Oh, look at his rosy cheeks!"

"So sweet!"

"The sisters of the night sense a virgin!"

Sam was frozen. He did not know what to say or do.

"Leave him alone," Vernon said, putting out his arm to make the three back off. "He hasn't come all this way to be badgered by the witches from Macbeth!"

"Don't be so cruel! Oh Vernon, don't be cruel!"

"Girls, girls, girls," said Stainton, shooing them away good naturedly. "My guest has just arrived and he'll be with us for some weeks. Plenty of time left to harass the poor soul."

The three weird sisters left Sam in good humour, each turning to wave extravagantly. It had been overwhelming. And his first encounter with homosexual transvestites.

Willy Diefenbaker was sitting outside the bar

with Max and Bruno in the evening sun. He felt increasingly ill at ease each visit now, realising how dangerous and stupid they really were. At first, he'd thought they were an asset to his and Vernon's business – a client reluctant to pay the agreed price for documents had to be threatened, after all. They had learned to keep pressure on customers who tried to negotiate a price less than agreed as well, like the one who'd sworn to send money back from Palestine after his safe arrival. Willy called him the optimistic escapee – not optimistic for very long, though.

But as prices increased, clients had become more desperate, and the risks of non-payment had compounded. Bruno and Max were more and more important to the business.

Although they fitted the bill as enforcers and collectors, they brought their own problems with them, and Willy suspected that they were criminally insane. Bruno particularly disturbed him, as he was not only psychotic but ambitious. He explained with barely contained glee how they'd tipped over the coffin and stamped on the woman's corpse, and their delighted laughter at the distress caused to the grieving son.

"He paid up quickly for the dead crone's passport then," Bruno crowed.

Willy wondered how best to caution them about their methods, but said nothing. They were dangerous young men, who could turn on employers if things weren't to their liking. Having accepted the money from them, paid their 'fee' with congratulations, he was anxious to get back inside the bar. Hopefully they'd then leave him for the night.

Unfortunately, they had other ideas, and Willy felt Bruno's firm grip on his forearm.

"Are you happy with us, Herr Diefenbaker?" he asked solemnly.

"Very happy," Willy lied.

"The highest form of joy there is on this earth is to make other people happy," Bruno said.

Willy was just about to thank them again, hoping it would encourage their departure, but he realised there was more.

"Who has had this joy in fuller measure than the Führer himself?" said Bruno. "The unhappiest people on whom God's sun shone have become the happiest in this wide world. Not one German in our great Fatherland would wish to be a member of another people or a citizen of another state. That for which all good Germans have always longed and hoped has now become reality under the blessed hand of the Führer: a single people in a great, free, and strong Reich."

"Heil Hitler," Max said.

Willy did not know what to say to words that were so eloquent, yet coming from the mouth of a buffoon.

He felt a chill down his spine. It was surreal. As if his pet cat had just picked up a camera and taken his photograph. Thankfully the other idiot twin went someway to righting the bizarre situation.

"The words are not his own, but they are well spoken," Max said. He nodded his admiration. "Well said, my brother."

"The words are not your own?" Willy asked. He hoped his tone would be taken as admiring curiosity and not the fear and contempt that he was feeling.

Bruno and Max were amused by the question.

"The words were spoken not three months ago on the date we met you. The glorious occasion of the Führer's birthday," Bruno explained.

"He was forty-nine years old on the 20th of April. He was born 1889," said Max.

Facts known to almost every other German.

Willy nodded.

"Very good," he said. He felt a growing desperation to go into the bar and mix with people with a measurable intelligence quota. But his arm was gripped again. Bruno had not finished.

"Perhaps it is also a religious act to put his whole life in the service of his people, and to work and act for the happiness of people," he intoned. "It is a religion without empty phrases and dogma, which nonetheless springs from the deepest depths of our soul. That is how our people understand it. We

Germans are today perhaps more faithful and pious than others who, though they never tire of praising God with their lips, have hearts that are cold and empty."

"Very, very good. Have you memorised the entire address?" Willy asked, trying to remember how long Goebbels' speech had been, and hoping Bruno hadn't.

"No, I have not. But in time I hope to, as does my brother. We also hope that such an accomplishment, together with your influential help, it will assist us in our gallant attempt to serve our Leader in our country's glorious army."

Willy Diefenbaker swallowed.

"As I have said before, my influence is limited in trying to gain your commissions." The twins chose to ignore such negativity.

"It will show those who once may have doubted us that we can learn subjects as well as being strong, loyal and dedicated soldiers." Max continued. "Shall we tell him now of our deeds to rid the streets of the vermin, brother?"

"Yes," said Bruno and the brothers nodded solemnly. Willy had no idea what was coming next, but felt that it would be anything but good.

"Since our arrival in Berlin, we have exterminated five Jewish rats," Max stated calmly. "In honour of our glorious Führer and our Fatherland."

Willy realised to his horror that he had to take

some responsibility for these murders. And while he had no sympathy with the victims, he feared sharply for his own safety. If he did not live up to the expectations of these insane twins, his life might also come to an abrupt end.

It was a little quieter inside the bar since the transvestites had left, but still lively, and Sam was enjoying himself. If his first few hours in Berlin were anything to go by, he was very much looking forward to the next few weeks. Vernon left him to see to other customers, and Herta took his place.

"Is the room to your satisfaction? she asked.
"Wonderful," he replied, "everything's just wonderful."

It was after one o' clock before he started to feel tired, but there was no sign of the music stopping or the drinks ceasing to flow. He thought that he'd take the following day off to acclimatise, perhaps, to talk to Vernon about a strategy.

Then start his railway travels after that.

ELEVEN

Helena, her father and Ralf visited the police station on a mission of hope. Not of receiving justice for Erna but for a decent and respectful burial. From the attitude of the sergeant in charge, they learned quickly that it was a fading hope. Jacob's standing in the community had once meant a great deal, but that was all gone now.

He knew he must adjust, curb his frustration, try to navigate his way through hostile, bewildering and impenetrable bureaucracy.

"Sergeant, you know me well. We have sat side by side on committees convened to ease the hardship this community has suffered over recent years. You know I was a prominent employer of local people and not just Jews. I employed many gentiles in my workforce. Paid good wages and treated everyone, no matter what creed or background, with respect."

The sergeant had once been happy himself to show respect to the businessman. Happy to have helped him on and off with his overcoat at meetings. He had once been subservient because his sons-in-law had worked at the furniture factory. The sergeant had been keen for them to do well, to get on and take over the financial burden of his daughters.

"All I ask now is not respect for myself, but respect for the poor young woman who lies dead in the morgue," Jacob pleaded.

The large, impassive policeman looked at the three people before him with contempt. And was surprised when the young man who looked like a nervous wreck started to speak.

"Respect, and pity upon her soul, that you may grant us permission to take her away for a burial by her people in a befitting religious ceremony," Ralf said.

"What are you mumbling at?" the sergeant asked, with derision. "Is it one of your incantations? Your whisperings to your unchristian God?"

"No, no, no sir," Jacob said, with self-disgust at having to almost disregard Ralf's despair and pander to the sergeant. "Our friend is in deep despair brought about by the terrible loss of his fiancée, his voice is weak with emotion. I speak for the three of us, pleading with you to allow us to take Erna away and bury her. That is all we ask."

"It is too much. You have no papers that would allow that to happen. You have no birth or death certificate. I do know you, Jacob Rosenhoff, and I also know that the young woman was your servant and not a blood relative. You may have had jurisdiction over her life, but not her afterlife. She is not your responsibility. We will dispose of the body unless the correct papers are produced."

"But I'm her fiancé," Ralf begged brokenly. "On the day she died we were leaving for America. How can I leave her?"

Helena consoled him as Jacob tried once more to reason with the policeman. "Sergeant, this is a monstrous situation. You know full well the circumstances that have brought us here. She left us that day and her intention was to travel to America with her fiancé where they were to be married. I request, in the strongest possible way, that decency prevails here and we can take her for burial."

The sergeant was becoming angry.

"You've tried my patience long enough," he shouted. "If there is more of this I will have you arrested, Rosenhoff."

"What? For what?" Jacob protested.

Helena, alarmed, left Ralf and was quickly at her father's side. "Please, sergeant. My father's only asking you to do the decent thing."

He ignored her.

"Rosenhoff, you may well have been a man of power and influence when you had a factory but that time has gone. You stand before me no more than an insolent Jew who wants me to break the laws I'm employed to enforce. Go, before I carry out my threat."

"I demand to see your superior," Jacob said, fighting with his temper.

"This must stop now! You must learn your place! Do not speak to me again!"

"Erna was more than a servant! She was a valued member of my household and my family. I cannot leave her where she is like a discarded item! She is not rubbish to be dumped! She is a human being, like you and me! I will see your superior officer! This madness must stop!"

Jacob had not lost control like this for years now, and he realised that his behaviour was unacceptable. The once proud and respected businessman breathed deeply as he composed himself. He waited for the inevitable reprisal.

"You are now under arrest," the sergeant said and signalled for another officer to join him.

Sam's mother had fretted daily since his departure. She'd never taken much interest in anything apart from her family's welfare, local news and neighbourhood gossip, but since her son had left home for the unknowns of the continent she had started to read her husband's newspaper.

In it, she read disturbing stories of great unrest. Sam's dad made light of Germany taking over Austria and Sudetenland, telling her it was quite reasonable as they were only protecting the rights of millions and millions of their own people who lived there. He dismissed her alarms about rearmament, explaining that Hitler's 'mob' had done a great job of modernising the country, and that making tanks and ships was a way of keeping people employed. Britain would not be dragged into any war, because everybody had learned so many bitter lessons from twenty years ago, and politicians were too clever to let it happen again. Trust our leaders, he reassured her. They're all far cleverer than we are.

There was great relief and joy when the letter arrived. Edith suggested that because it was a Monday with Gwen and Edgar coming for tea they should delay the opening until then, but mother had ripped open the envelope before Edith had finished her sentence. However, as she read it, she did agree that it would be a nice thing if Edith read it aloud to all later.

There had been no announcement, just a conspiratorial shared smile between mother and daughter as they cleared away the dishes. Then, after manufacturing some intrigue, Edith took the letter from behind the clock on the mantelpiece. She cleared her throat theatrically.

"We've had a letter from our Sam which I will

now read to all that's interested," she said delightedly.

"I've already read it," mother said, lest anybody thought her maternal instincts might be wanting.

"He's all right, isn't he?" Gwen asked.

"He's fine."

"I bet he's even cockier than a week ago," Edgar said. "Will you all just shut up and listen!" their father bellowed. Edith began to read:

Dear everybody back in boring Doncaster.

"Told you!" Edgar said, as the others shushed him. "God only knows what he's going to be like when he gets back."

I hope you're all well as I am. Berlin is great and my digs are top class. I'm above a bar that only seems to shut in the middle of the night, but before you say it, mother, I'm in bed at a decent hour. Vernon, the man who's looking after me, is a good sort. It's difficult to work out his job as he seems to spend a lot of time in the bar and in bed, but I suppose he must do a lot behind the scenes that I don't know about. The people are very friendly and happy. The weather is great so they spend a lot of time outside and there is singing and dancing almost every night.

Food is different but enjoyable and beer very good but expensive compared to home. I've spent the last four days travelling on the railways and Vernon is happy with my reports. I have come across some who are grumbling about politics and fear for the future but you get them everywhere and, on the whole, the majority are much like home.

Two days ago, I took the train to Hanover which is the chief manufacturing base of armaments. It was very busy and I was very impressed with my journey and overnight stay.

Everything I've seen so far seems to be clean and very modern. The roads are wide and straight, the buildings bright, and if they are a government or post office, they usually have a black and red flag attached. Some of them are huge.

From what I have seen of the railway system I have been impressed by diesel engines, and it would not surprise me if Sir Nigel took us in that direction soon, although they lack the character of something like the Mallard. *To me A4 Pacifics are more like a tamed beast snorting steam and having its power restrained, like a stallion trying to break free of its bridle. The diesels can never be like that, but it is a lot less hardship for the crew.*

I'll sign off now. It's Friday and I'm missing mam's finny haddy followed by rhubarb pie, but it won't be long before I'm back to eat with you and telling you all my news in person. I'll write again next week. Ask Edgar to let me know any news from work and the cricket scores. Best wishes to all.

Yours,
Sam.

"That's it. Seems like he only posted it three days ago. Imagine that. From Berlin to Doncaster so quickly," Edith said, displaying the post mark on the envelope.

"Can I have the stamp?" asked Edgar.

"What for?" said Gwen.

"One of the lads at work collects them. Mad about it. Reckons he's got a better collection than the King. Mind you, he also says he bowls a better off-break than Arnold Hamer!"

"So then, our Sam seems all right, anyway," dad said. He'd taken the letter from Edith to read himself.

"Yes, he does." Mother was satisfied and relieved. She stood to dish out the pudding.

"He's talking rot about diesel though," said Mr Bolton. "It'll never replace steam until our coal runs out. In about a thousand years!"

"Well, you can argue that point when he gets home. Funny he should mention finny haddy with it not being his favourite, though. I hope he's not fretting for his food and he's eating all right."

"Course he'll be eating all right, Mam. He eats like a horse wherever he is," Gwen told her.

"He might actually be eating horses," said Edgar, putting his spoon back in his empty pudding bowl. "You know what it's like abroad."

"I ate horse in Belgium during the war, and I was glad of it," dad said and mother smiled, knowing what was coming next. "The best bit is from the base of the neck, top side, not underneath. An officer told me that when I was on guard duty."

"Well, we'll be happy to take your word for it and be happy with our home-grown beef. Our Sam doesn't seem to think there'll be another war. That's one good thing of him being over there seeing for himself." Mam said, looking on the bright side.

"Aye, we've all had enough of that. Us and them," said dad reflectively. Such memories always sent him into a quiet spell.

"I'll write back, shall I," Edith said brightly. "What messages do you want to send?"

"Tell him there's going to be brake trials using the *Mallard* a week on Friday."

"Work? That's a bit boring, Edgar," Gwen said. She started helping her mother clear the table.

"Not to Sam," laughed Edgar. "He'll know they'll be going for the world speed record soon after. And he'll be sad to miss it."

TWELVE

"Will they come for you, papa?" Helena asked, moving her hands under the table so as not to let her father see them shaking with fear.

"No. Not if I do as I am bid and report daily to the police station," Jacob replied.

He had been taken away after his outburst, and treated roughly in a holding cell, receiving no answers to his questions and objections. After a terrible hour of uncertainty Helena and Ralf had been told to go home. No amount of pleading led to any explanation of what was happening to Jacob Rosenhoff.

"Report for how long?" Helena forced herself to ask.

"Until they tell me not to."

Helena realised the strain on him was more than she had first noticed. Sitting at the table, head bowed with the low light accentuating the worry lines on his face, he seemed to be ageing a month for every day their suffering continued. Somehow, she must persuade him to act on the information gained from Ralf.

"Until they tell you not to report daily?"

"Yes," he said. "The law is proving to be very

flexible for us these days." He was trying to make light of his plight; but he failed miserably.

Helena knew she would have to tread lightly to persuade him to do as she wanted. He could be very stubborn, and her suggestion would mean committing a crime. Even though authorities now took outrageous liberties in their interpretation of the law, Jacob Rosenhoff still believed that acting within society's rules was their best chance of survival. However, even his hopes for a return to security and contentment were quickly fading.

"Ralf told me where he obtained papers to leave the country, papa. If we are to guarantee our safety, we must do the same."

"I assumed he went through the necessary, laborious procedures."

"No, he did not."

"So where did he obtain them?"

"From an Englishman who has a bar in the Kurfürstendam." Helena told him, and waited for his reaction. "He bypassed the system for expediency."

"What on earth was he doing exposing himself to illegal activity?" Although he knew full well.

"He was doing his best to secure a safe passage. As we must. You have to attend the conference in Évian. You have to spread the word about the evil in this city, in our country. To do that you must leave it."

"Yes, but we must also keep our heads, and behave

properly. I must not repeat my foolish action of appealing to their last shreds of decency. That poor child's body. What will happen to it now, Helena?"

"I don't know, I truly don't, papa. But we must make your safety our priority. Because of our sense of decency and love for Erna we have put ourselves in jeopardy. I fear the knock at any time, day or night. I fear evil at our door, and the willing slaves of evil taking you away."

Uncharacteristically, Jacob did not know what to say or do, which unnerved his daughter. All her life he had been a man who made the decisions about his business and family matters with the utmost certainty. She looked at him in his weakened state. His shoulders stooped and bright eyes dulled. She had to be his strength. She had to drive their escape from barbarism.

"I don't know what we can do," he said. "Erna's body still lies in the morgue and we have no hope of giving her a proper burial. With my interference, I have put us both in danger. By my naïve pleading."

"Which is what any decent man would have done in the situation," she said. "Erna would understand and forgive us and we must flee. Papa, that is what we must now do."

"Where to, Helena. Where to?"

"We've known people who have left. They've written back to say they're safe. In America, Great

Britain, other places. We must do it, papa. You and everyone capable must go and tell the world how we're being treated, persecuted. There must be an intervention before this madness becomes truly catastrophic."

Ralf's body had been hanging from the rafters of his attic apartment for three days before it was discovered. His landlord, more concerned about overdue rent than his tenant's welfare, had let himself into the sparse accommodation, fearing the young man had fled without paying. Ralf had been a reliable tenant for a few years, but recently he had given and withdrawn his notice, alerting the landlord to the possibility of being out of pocket.

The landlord had searched the suicide victim for cash before alerting the authorities of his grisly find, caring nothing about Ralf's motivations. His priority was to be rid of the corpse and render the rooms fit for occupation as soon as possible.

Likewise, the morgue attendants were ignorant of the fact that Ralf's lifeless body was placed on the same slab recently occupied by his deceased fiancée Erna. She had been unceremoniously despatched to an unmarked grave, a fate awaiting Ralf once the paperwork had been completed. No one would ever know if the two young lovers would be buried together, completing a tragic romantic twist of fate.

Helena found out about the death while buying bread. The news saddened but did not shock the community, as a cloud of inevitable despair hung over them all semi-permanently. However, it did galvanise her. She had been encouraging her father to liquidate his assets as best he could without drawing attention to themselves. His business and property was no longer his own but he had converted some goods into cash over the previous months, while other valuables or family heirlooms that could be easily transported had been carefully hidden away.

When Helena told him the bad news, they decided it was time to go. There had been a shifting in their relationship, and her decisions and actions were now considered equal to her father's. She resolved to act without consulting him on some important matters for the first time in her life. She was going to make preliminary enquiries at the bar where Ralf had obtained travel documents for himself and Erna.

It was outside in the sunshine that she met Sam Bolton.

THIRTEEN

Encouraged by the weather and his boss, Sam had decided to take a day off from travelling the railways, and enjoy the company in the bar. He had taken to playing chess with his patron, and the two of them enjoyed it as a competition of equals. Sam knew that if they played later in the day he would always win, given Vernon's consumption of brandy and subsequent cavalier attitude in his tactics but Sam, being fair-minded, encouraged play no later than mid-morning when it was still a level playing field.

They sat outside in the sunshine watching passers-by go about their business as they played their game. Sam had been taught by his mother from an early age. She had been taught by an uncle, and since his death had been keen for an opponent as her husband and her other children were not interested. Vernon Stainton's coach had been a Russian émigré, a maths tutor at his prep school, and if he never got a game at all it would not have troubled him. His attitude to chess matched his attitude to life. He had been privileged in his education, but had squandered it and settled for an easy dissolution.

The game was interrupted as both men noticed the dark-haired, attractive woman stop outside the bar. She looked tentative as she checked the address on a note she'd taken from her purse. She wore a smart summer dress, hat, white gloves and carried a small bag which could not have held much more than the purse she tucked back into it.

Sam was reminded of the woman he'd seen with her family at the underground back in London. She was younger, and unencumbered with children, but looked almost as strained. There was a vulnerability about her which made him feel protective, but at the same time attracted. He watched as she tried to look in through the windows without making herself too obvious. Passing their table, she smiled apologetically, realising that her shadow was across the chess board, and Sam smiled back, considering whether to speak to her or not. Helena too was hesitant, but decided the situation by walking away.

Sam was sorry to see her leave, quite clearly. And Vernon thought to counsel him.

"Don't get involved with her sort," he said, concentrating on the board.

"You mean a very attractive young woman?"

"I mean a Jew."

Sam watched as Helena walked away. She was dressed demurely, and her slightly bowed head gave the impression that she did not want to be noticed. But he couldn't take his eyes off her. He had found her apologetic smile for blocking out the sun quite captivating. But he was puzzled by Vernon's attitude and his certainty.

"How do you know that she's a Jew?" he asked, as she distanced herself from them. "Sam, you're so young and inexperienced. I know a Jew when I see one, and I'm surprised you don't." He moved his queen out of danger. "You must have seen one before."

"I don't know that I have," said Sam. "I wouldn't know a catholic, a protestant, a Methodist or whatever else anybody might be if I didn't know them personally. I've never really thought about it."

"Back home you don't have to. But here and now it's best to know who's who, and that's a fact. Are you going to make your move?"

"I wouldn't really know what to say," Sam said, with some regret. "Not being able to speak German."

"I meant the game. Come on, I'm going to win this."

Sam concentrated on the board, and made an unexpected move with his bishop that took Vernon by surprise. The game was in the balance and both gave the outcome their full attention. In the short time they had known each other they'd found almost nothing in common, but nevertheless had enjoyed each other's company. Vernon liked teasing Sam about his working-class background, his Yorkshire accent and (until leading him astray), his work ethic.

For Sam, how someone so privileged and well educated could have ended up in charge of a bar in a foreign capital was the fascination. How could someone be so totally devoid of ambition? How could he have so easily left his family, friends and country? How could he have so physically let himself go, existing on brandy and irregular snacks forced on him by Herta?

"She's coming back," Sam said as he looked into the near distance while waiting for Vernon to make his move.

"Who?"

"The very attractive young woman who looks lost."

"Oh, the Jew," said Vernon. He countered a new offensive by threatening a knight with a pawn.

"Why do you say it like that? Disdainfully, I mean."

"If you don't know them, if you have never had any dealings with them, then you're not to know, I suppose. But when you're somewhat older and far more experienced, you'll know them for what they are."

"Which is what?"

"Parasites who live on the backs of hard-working people all over the world. A race who make money out of money. Shakespeare personified the Jewish ethic in Shylock. Have you read much of the Bard?"

"Not a word. Anyway, how do you know for certain that she is Jewish?"

"Oh Samuel, you naive Tyke—" He broke off. "Check."

Vernon had countered the threat to his king by moving his queen into attack. He went on, "I can guarantee that she, a Jew, when watching you and I play this innocent game would only see an opportunity for profit."

Sam smiled at the thought. Which he found ridiculous.

"You may smile," said Stainton, "but her sort would seek and find a way to monetise it. Not by gambling, they're too shrewd for that, but by charging for the table, say, or the board, or for spectators to watch. Something like that."

Sam laughed, until he realised Vernon was serious.

"Vernon," he pointed out, uncomfortably, "It's your board, your table, and there are no spectators."

"Then the Jew would charge rent for the pavement. They'd find a way. Do not underestimate their greed."

Sam was almost speechless.

"Vernon, that's the most ridiculous thing I have ever heard. And it disappoints me to listen to a man of obvious intelligence talk such rubbish. Oh my

God, she's coming back."

Helena had made her mind up that she must be brave and take the next step. She must enter the bar, convinced that salvation lay within. Sam watched her approach. Her hair was jet black and pulled back from her face, falling to one side on her neck. Her hat cast a shadow over her eyes. She was slim and perhaps no more than five feet four inches in flat shoes. The sleeves of her floral-patterned dress finished at her elbows, and white gloves might be hiding a wedding ring, which Sam found intriguing.

Not wanting to seem forward by gazing directly at her, he looked down at the chessboard, anticipating her arrival in about ten seconds. He had the choice of either capturing Vernon's pawn, or sacrificing his rook and hoping it would be taken for a lapse of concentration and lure him into a trap.

"Heil Hitler," Vernon said abruptly, taking him by surprise. The salutation was directed at Helena, and Sam wondered why she had not made the almost reflex response. Instead, she looked flustered, her naturally pale complexion colouring with embarrassment, and he felt uncomfortable to be part of the cause of it. Helena nodded briefly, then turned and walked away.

"See, she didn't say it." Vernon was quietly triumphant and turned back to the game, until he realised Sam was looking at him uncomprehendingly.

"If they're Jewish they can't respond. It's the law, and a damn good way of telling just who's who. Although some are devious, of course, and say it. They're taking a risk though."

Vernon realised he was talking to himself. Sam had left the table and was walking towards Helena.

"Excuse me, Fraülein. I can't speak German, I'm English. Sorry." Having caught up with her he was feeling faintly stupid.

"What do you want?" Helena answered in perfect English, which took him by surprise.

"I don't want anything. Well, I want to help if you need any assistance. I am sorry to approach you like this but you seem to be a little lost." Lots of people were passing in all directions and the traffic was quite heavy but Sam was not aware of any distraction. His focus was all on the attractive woman in front of him.

Helena was embarrassed that she had brought notice to herself, but relieved in a way. The English man's intrusion had made her focus again on what she had to do. She must complete her mission, as alien to her nature as it was. She realised that the Englishman was speaking to her again. She found him refreshingly open and while he was definitely bold in his approach there was an innocence about his manner.

"Can I help in any way? Not that I know my way

around the city, being English ... as I've already said," he said smiling apologetically. Helena thought him kind and decided she would trust him.

"I am looking for an Englishman."

She said it just loud enough for him to hear.

"Are you really?" Sam asked, quite surprised

"Yes. Might you be Vernon Stainton?"

"No, I'm afraid not," Sam said and she could not help but look disappointed. "That's him over there. At the table."

He'd hoped she would be pleased with the information, but Helena was not impressed. She'd taken an instant dislike to the fat tormentor who'd said "Heil Hitler" in such a provocative way.

Sam considered that she was even more attractive than at first sight. She had dark sparkling eyes, a neat nose, perfectly shaped lips and high cheekbones. She was probably the most beautiful woman he had ever met, and he did not want her to leave.

"Shall I introduce you to Vernon?" he asked. He had no idea why the young woman would want to meet the middle-aged reprobate, but he was keen to oblige.

She looked hesitant, and to put her more at ease he smiled and introduced himself. "I'm Sam by the way, Sam Bolton. I must say that your English is very good. You put me to shame."

She could not help but be taken by his

straightforward manner and she relaxed a little. But not enough to trust him with her full name.

"I am Helena."

"Come on then, Helena," Sam said, and encouraged her to walk with him back to the table where Vernon was wondering what was happening. The older man scowled and looked unapproachable, and Sam's instinct was to take her hand to reassure her. But sensing it might scare her away, he just gave his friendliest smile. A few steps and they were standing by the chessboard.

"Vernon," he said, "this young lady would like to make your acquaintance."

"Would she now?"

Vernon said it as if it were no surprise to him whatsoever, which surprised Sam. He tried again.

"Vernon, this is Helena. Helena, this is Vernon Stainton."

They exchanged a brief handshake. Vernon did not stand up, and stared at her in what Sam considered a rather impolite way.

"What can I do for you?" he said.

"I need your help." Helena said impassively leaving Sam wondering what Vernon could possibly do for her. She was an unlikely candidate to be a barmaid.

"To travel?" Vernon asked.

"Yes."

Vernon stood, and headed for the entrance to the bar. "Come inside," he said, coldly. "Checkmate, by the way."

It was such an afterthought, that Sam looked at the board to confirm it. Indeed, his king had no safe haven. When he looked up again, Vernon and Helena had disappeared and he was left feeling rather foolish.

Max Schafer broke a silence that had lasted for almost a minute.

"We could crucify him, I suppose," he said.

"Why?" Bruno asked.

"Because that's what his people did to Our Lord Jesus Christ."

Bruno nodded his grave agreement, but felt they needed to be practical.

"You're right Max, but it would not be easy. Timber, nails, the space to do it properly. And we might be caught by people who didn't understand our reasoning. Better not. We must find another way."

"See him squirm as he listens to us, though. Like a cow in the slaughterhouse. They always know."

"They do," his twin agreed.

The man tied and gagged in the chair knew all right. He knew he was in mortal danger. He had known from the moment he had opened his door, before they'd entered and knocked him to the ground with relentless ferocity. He had scrambled to get to his knees in an effort to stand, but the kicks and blows prevented him. His glasses had fallen and been crushed under a heel. He had viewed his kitchen from unnatural angles, as his head had been violently twisted and jammed against the base of the cupboard spilling tins of food that fell on him. It was not until the frenzy of the initial attack had subsided had he known why the madness was happening to him in his own home.

Beaten into submission, tied and gagged on his favourite kitchen chair, he was told why. He was a Jew. For that reason and no other, he was about to be killed by two men he had never seen before. They had picked him out from a group of people leaving a synagogue. It was not personal; they would have killed anyone who happened to be at that place, at that time. It was because they were strong, ruthless, and insane. And wanting to impress Herr Willy Diefenbaker.

"Do you want to slit his throat, Max? As you would a filthy pig in the sty," Bruno asked. "Or should I do it?"

"No, I'll do it, but first I'll stab his heart to prevent blood spurting from a severed artery and covering me in it. The butcher's apron from home would be useful."

"You're being very wise, Max. We've a distance to travel back to our apartment. Evidence of this slaughter would be unwanted."

Max opened drawers to search for a suitable weapon of execution. The victim's eyes grew wider with terror, his wrists strained against the thin rope that bound them and, try as he might, he failed to utter anything but a strangled squeal from his gagged mouth.

FOURTEEN

Sam stayed outside in the sunshine when Vernon and Helena went into the bar. Customers were filling the place up as lunchtime approached, and he nodded and smiled to some he recognised as regulars. Shortly afterwards, Helena looked at him briefly as she stepped back onto the pavement and turned to walk away. She looked so upset, he decided to go after her. It was against his nature to be so spontaneous but her attraction was overwhelming.

"Helena?" he said, as he caught up with her. She turned to look, but did not stop. She was obviously not impressed to see who had accosted her. "I know we've only just met – well, hardly that! But are you all right?"

"Yes. I am fine."

"You're clearly not. Stop a moment. Maybe I can help."

"And why would you want to do that?" she asked. She had ventured out to try and improve her and her father's situation but had failed to do so. She may have made things much worse, in fact, and now this young Englishman was interfering. Who was he? How could he possibly help? A foreign stranger. She was aware that he was still speaking to her.

"I don't know, I just want …" Sam said.

"What? To take advantage of me?" Her aggressive attitude surprised her, and she immediately regretted the words, seeing his reaction.

"Now that is just uncalled for!" said Sam. "If you're going to be like that I'll just leave you to it."

Helena stopped. She took a breath, composed herself.

"You work with Herr Stainton, do you?

"I suppose so. Sort of."

She had to find out if he was a waste of time. Or, possibly, could even help.

"Are you going to make me a better offer?" she said, oddly. She had mustered up enough spirit to make the tears in her eyes shine with defiance.

Sam had no idea what she meant.

"A better offer. How do you mean?"

"Herr … Mr Stainton's … demands were so outrageous, and then you offer to help in the street. In return for …" She could not go on.

Sam sensed her vulnerability. That she was feigning confidence but was out of her depth. In whatever the business with Vernon might have been.

"For what?" he asked again. "In return for what?"

"Favours," she blurted. "Oh, I don't know! Perhaps I've totally misjudged you. I'm so worried, terrified, there's … I just don't know what to do."

On the pavement, in the street, Helena broke down and cried. Instinctively, Sam took her gently by the shoulders.

"I've no idea what you are talking about," he said, "but I want to know. Helena, will you please tell me? Maybe, just maybe, I can help."

She looked at him.

Willy was enjoying a quiet early evening drink. Vernon had told him of the pretty young Jewess who'd approached him in search of passports and papers. The men had laughed at her reaction to sexual favours being part of the transaction. Diefenbaker thoroughly approved of his partner's outrageous suggestions, because there might be something in it for him. Vernon had gone upstairs promising to return soon, and his last words were about Helena and how pretty she was. It was that thought that was pleasing Willy as he nursed his beer and enjoyed the peace. Moments later all that was shattered as his name was whispered in his ear.

"Herr Diefenbaker?"

Willy turned to see the crazy twins looking impassively at him. He tried to hide his horror.

"Good evening, my friends. To what do I owe this pleasure?" Bruno and his brother stood almost to attention.

"We have two things which we think may impress you."

"What are these impressive things?" Willy asked unenthusiastically.

"The first is my brother's progress regarding the memorisation of the speech given at our beloved Führer's birthday celebrations," Bruno said. "A further recitation from the address of Joseph Goebbels."

Willy desperately willed Vernon to appear, or the ground to engulf him. But neither happened, and Max intoned the promised text:

"How moving it was as he crossed the Innsbruck bridge, entering his hometown and birthplace Braunau, for the first time in many years. We saw pictures in the newspapers of women giving him flowers as he stepped on Austrian soil. The eyes of these women shone with the deepest and purest joy, such that one cannot imagine more beautiful human faces. We saw a picture of a man who climbed onto the Führer's automobile with his hands raised as if in prayer, and we had the sense that here the depths of the human soul came to the most perfect expression …"

Max came to a hesitant stop, and Willy forced himself to look impressed, as he nodded sombrely.

"Probably never before have the hearts …" Bruno

prompted, and Willy realised that there was more to come, and looked happy in anticipation. He was anything but.

"Probably never before have the hearts of all Germans beat faster or more passionately than in these afternoon and evening hours. The nation knew that the Führer was on the soil of our German Austria, and never did his beloved voice seem warmer and nearer than on this evening, when he spoke in Linz for the first time in his homeland. Hundreds and hundreds of kilometres from us, and yet near to us all, he spoke of the joy that filled his heart."

Max had finished his recitation, and was proud of his achievement. He looked at Willy for a reaction.

The gap in time between the end of the speech and Willy applauding lightly was interpreted as emotion stifling his brain. In reality he was switching it back on. He had to, somehow, get them out of his life.

"And the second thing, Herr Diefenbaker …" Bruno reminded.

He prayed it was not more of the speech, but Bruno was unwrapping something in a newspaper. At first glance Willy did not recognise what he was being shown. Bruno held it as if it were a prize, and Max looked on with pride. Slowly, it dawned on Diefenbaker what he was looking at. It was a heart, and as he hoped it was not human, the twins were quick to disabuse him.

"We did it correctly, using skills we learned from our parents," Bruno said. "Our father could kill even the largest beast with a blade no bigger than this …" He indicated about six inches, but Willy could hardly take in what he was being told. He indicated for the heart to be rewrapped and moved away from him.

"First we stabbed the heart which stopped its function, and when the throat was cut no blood was pumped out from the severed artery," Max informed him calmly.

Willy feared the answer, but he had to ask.

"Whose heart is … whose heart was it?"

"Just a Jew," they said in unison.

"One less, and one more to put us in good favour with you and our glorious army," added Bruno.

"We are ready to serve as commanded," Max said, and the twins stood tall, their chests inflated with pride.

"Will you speak up for us soon?" asked Bruno. They looked at him for approval of their latest display of nationalist loyalty.

"Yes, yes of course," Willy blustered. He fought to be calm, to somehow take charge of the crazy situation. "You have proved your worth and your skills. This can now be stopped. In fact, it must be stopped. No more killing. No more violence."

"Unless you have more debts for us to collect

and it becomes necessary once more," Bruno said reasonably.

Willy Diefenbaker nodded helplessly.

"Perhaps under certain circumstances. But will you both give assurance that you won't kill again just randomly?" He wished he had never engaged them in conversation. He knew that he'd been swept along with the fervour of the Führer's birthday, like everybody at the rally. God knows why the twin killers had latched on to him, but they had and now it had turned into a nightmare. He must be rid, but how?

"We will obey your commands without question," Bruno said. "There will be no more killings if you're satisfied that we have proved our worth."

"Yes, you have, you have. Believe me, young fellows, I am totally convinced of your great worth."

His smile was fixed and forced. The twins looked back impassively.

Willy would have to give up on being rescued by Vernon. He would drink up soon, check his watch, be amazed at how time flies and make his excuses to leave. All relatively easy.

But he must find a permanent solution to rid him of these unwanted disciples.

Permanent, and soon.

FIFTEEN

Sam read the letter from home for the second time. It was good to catch up with everyone, and he'd been looking forward to finding out the cricket scores, but the distance from home had made him less interested rather than more, which surprised him. He was very interested to hear about the *Mallard* brake trials, though, and realised the significance – it meant that Sir Nigel Gresley would definitely be attempting the world speed record.

Sam was sorry to be missing that. He knew that if a steam engine could take the record from a diesel the ramifications would be enormous; steam would be king for the foreseeable future. But strangely, even this excited him less than he'd expected. The world speed record for a locomotive was in the grasp of his company, and the *Mallard* no less, but…

He also knew the reason for his distraction. It was Helena. After he'd caught up with her, they had walked on. They'd stopped at a café and sat outside, and they could have been two lovers planning their future. Instead she was a distraught young woman fearful for her and her father's life, and he a bewildered ignoramus.

Sam listened with increasing sympathy and

horror as the story unfolded. He felt powerless, but determined to help in some way. He also realised that in the short time he had spent with Helena she was like no other person he had ever met before.

His sister Gwen had often teased him that he would know when the right one came along, and he had joked that she had drawn the short straw if her 'right one' was Edgar. Gwen and Edgar had grown up only a few streets apart, attended the same school, seen a lot of each other before starting their serious courting. Now here was Sam thinking he might be smitten by somebody he'd only spent a few hours with.

And that was under strange circumstances, encompassing his rapid education about the plight of a persecuted minority. His mind was in a turmoil.

"Listen to me young man," said Vernon Stainton, "and listen well for your own sake. Stay in the shallow end. In fact, don't even dip your toe into the pool."

Sam's expression told Vernon he had to speak more directly to his guest. There was a lack of understanding.

"You have no idea what's going on over here," he continued, "except for little bits of information you've picked up on your train journeys. Well, stick to that, it's all that's being asked of you. In a couple of weeks, you'll be back in Blighty. Back in that drawing office of yours impressing your chums and making them jealous about your exploits here in Germany. Enjoy the rest of your time and don't get involved."

He paused, to see if it was sinking in.

"I've told you about the Jews, haven't I? She'll exploit you given less than half a chance, that's what they do, it's what they've always done. Stick to what you came here for, and I'll bet my assessment of you won't do any harm for your career. Now then, what about this steam engine world record bid? What is going to happen then?"

"I'm surprised that you're interested," Sam said. He was disappointed with Vernon's dismissal of Helena's plight, and hoped he had merely misread the situation, not understood the seriousness of her request, the urgency of getting her father to the conference in France. He did not fully understand it himself, but knew instinctively she was desperate for help. Her sadness at the deaths of her friend and the mistreatment at the hands of the police had alarmed him considerably. He was determined to do all he could.

But Vernon was dismissive.

"Willy was asking, that's all," he said.

"About what, exactly?" Sam said. "What's the interest?"

"Well, this speed record attempt. Bit of flat track, is it? Grantham; Lincolnshire. I've been there, or nearby I think. Your steam engine back home. What's it called, the *Mallard*?"

"Yes. Yes, it is. But I'm not sure if you should have discussed it with Willy."

"He's interested, that's all. Proud of their *Flying Hamburger* or whatever it's called, he's just overly patriotic – the Germans are. There's no cloak-and-dagger stuff with Willy."

He went behind the bar to refill his brandy glass, and Sam knew he had to change the subject back to Helena. "He is your partner in the passport business though, isn't he?"

Vernon was suddenly alarmed.

"I think Herta might be talking to you about things she knows damn all about," he said defensively. "The passport business is at the behest of our government. It's a sensitive area."

"Have you forgotten telling me that Willy was a valuable aid in your transport venture? Yourself? Two nights ago, when you'd received a big payment from those twin brothers. Your pocket bulged with cash and you asked me to help count it. I told you it was dangerous to be so drunk in charge of so much money."

"Sam, have you forgotten there's a chain of command in this bar operation, and you're at the bottom? Whatever game I play, whatever I choose as my landlord persona, is not to be questioned by anybody, okay? Especially an interloper such as you. Is that clear, my young and inexperienced friend?"

Sam knew it was time to speak up for himself, and for his principles. He had known within a few hours of meeting Vernon that he was not the man that he pretended. This drunk was no Scarlet Pimpernel, no deft secret operator working for the good of the King's Government and the British people and all they stood for: he was merely a self-serving drunk. A clever man, no doubt, but a privileged, well-educated waster.

Everything about him, now, had become anathema to Sam's lifestyle and work ethic, and it was Helena who had given him a wake-up call. So far, he had lived cocooned in a safe, predictable environment ignorant of world affairs. But life did not stop at Yorkshire's boundaries. He knew how close to dire peril England had become.

"I do know my place," he said. "But surely the purpose of your operation here is to help endangered Jewish people leave the city for a safer, better life? I know that Helena has told you how vital it is for her father to attend an international conference in France, organised by America. People will listen to him, and it's important. You must know what is going on in this city, and that we've got to help?"

Still Stainton showed no anger.

"I help them all the time," he said. "You're a

newcomer here, you'll soon be on your way. Don't pretend you know anything, all right?"

"I know what she has told me," Sam said, determined to hold his ground.

Now Vernon patronised. "Sam, Sam, Sam," he smiled. "She's recognised a Yorkshire tyke, okay, still wet behind the ears. Enough of this now. Attend to your own business. You must have a report to write."

"I've told her that it is my business, that I'll make sure it is. She must have the necessary documents, Vernon. She must."

"Oh don't be silly, young man. Unlike you, I know exactly what I'm doing." Vernon's glass had been drained and refilled again. He rejoined Sam on the customer side of the bar.

"And so do I, now." Sam was growing in confidence. "You're demanding an exorbitant amount of cash from Helena and her father. And you've asked for something more, that is despicable. Can you deny that, Vernon?"

Vernon found such straight questioning difficult. It was potentially dangerous, also. His masters knew he would be skimming some of the cream from the operation, and would turn a blind eye to it. However, they would be more than annoyed if they found out how much he was actually making.

Sam drove his point home.

"Asking for sexual favours." he said, bluntly.

"Blackmail. I can't see that being condoned by the British Government, can you?"

Vernon saw Sam in a new light. Still naïve, but young and fit, with bravery shining in his determined face. But Vernon had been in many a similar situation before, and he had never failed to talk his way out of it.

"I didn't know you'd started a holiday romance with the gal," he chuckled. "Good luck to you I say, Sam – but it's a free market and you can't blame me for chancing my arm. As for the sexual favours, can you blame me for employing any advantage I might have on that score? I've got something she desperately wants, and she's got something I wouldn't mind a piece of at all. If we can come to a mutually beneficial arrangement, all well and good, not true?"

He did not wait for a reaction.

"I wouldn't criticise you for using your youth and good looks would I, Sam – so why should you criticise me for using my influence in high places. I'll bet the King's brother himself chuckled when he found out who he'd shared a mistress with. Only yours truly! Oh come on, come on, let's get Herta to knock us up a little snack. But not a word about the hanky-panky, okay? She can be a fiery jealous woman when it takes her."

"No, Vernon! You don't get to fob me off so easily. If it's in your power to help Helena and her father escape, then you must do it."

He was unperturbed.

"All right Sam, I'll see what I can do. But you've got no idea of the complexities of my operation here, I'm telling you. It isn't just a matter of taking cash and supplying papers; I have to consider the reaction of the authorities in every individual case.

"That's where Willy comes in. He gives me the inside track on what the party will say. Please don't interfere, because the consequences could be disastrous.

"Stick to the trainspotting, old man. Now, let me get you a big drink."

SIXTEEN

Vernon was nowhere near convinced that he'd persuaded Sam not to rock the boat. He'd had to admit he'd underestimated the young Yorkshireman, and judged him by his own low standards. Sam would treat the whole escapade as a lark, he'd thought, overindulge himself in everything on offer, and return home with many a bacchanalian tale to tell. But the bloody trainspotter was a conscientious worker, who had written good reports which Vernon had had to put into code and send back to the 'brewery' in London.

Now he'd fallen under the spell of a Jewess, an attractive one at that, which could only cause more trouble. What a pain. And Diefenbaker, his partner in the money-making venture, was also bringing problems. "Calm down, Willy," he'd told him. "Can't you just get them placed into the army and have done with it?"

"Of course, I can't. Don't you think I would have done if it was that easy? They're psychopaths. Killers with no sympathy at all for their victims. My real fear is they'll turn on me, Vernon. When I fail to do as promised."

"And what exactly would that be, then?"

Vernon knew full well that Willy's problem was also his.

"I hinted that I'd help them to enlist. Perhaps as commissioned officers. I talked big to get them as our debt collectors, but I didn't expect them to kill just to impress me. *Our* debt collectors, Vernon. *Our* thugs. Not just mine."

"All right, Willy, I get the point." Vernon hated anything that disrupted his laissez-faire lifestyle: he hated alarm clocks, reporting in, having to be reliable; but most of all he hated having to solve other people's problems. It should just be a German matter, with Willy solving it himself. Instead, Vernon would have to come up with an answer.

"What a pain," he said. "I've got more than enough on my mind at the moment with my bloody Yorkshire do-gooder. Insubordination, that's his game."

The two men fell silent as they thought through the situation.

"We could get the twins to kill your trainspotter, I suppose," Diefenbaker offered, without much enthusiasm. "Then somehow have them arrested. Solving both problems."

"And shine the spotlight on us? I'm not the only British agent in Berlin am I, Willy, and people would start snooping around. No, we need to be cleverer than that." He paused. "But you have sparked the old imagination, though, my friend."

"How so?" asked Willy, hopefully.

"Let me just ponder a while," said Vernon. He felt enthusiasm growing for his embryonic plan.

"And this business of the speed record," put in Willy. "I must report it. Germany must retain it at all costs."

Vernon shook his head in disbelief at the irrelevance of his colleague.

"Don't be so silly, man," he said. "Let history take its course for God's sake. Suppose Blighty takes it from your Fatherland – so what? Germany will probably take it back again some time, and anyway that's for others to worry about. Let's concentrate on solving our complications, and not worry about people playing with their bloody train sets."

Willy said stiffly: "Our railways are a source of great national pride. I'd be failing badly in my duty as a loyal citizen if I did nothing and let your country steal away our glory."

Vernon shook his head slowly. He felt a ton of trouble on his shoulders.

Helena had met Sam at Potsdamer Bahnhof as arranged. He had made an early start from the bar and travelled towards Aachen, studying the heavy industry along the way. On his journey back he had written a detailed report on what he'd seen, to finish later in his room. It was plain to him that Germany was capable of waging war imminently. He had grave doubts that England could avoid involvement.

At the station café, he and Helena drank coffee, and she said her father wanted to meet him. Under ordinary circumstances any new male friend of his daughter would have been possibly suspect, but in these extraordinary times even those considered friends could be dangerous betrayers. Jacob was extremely wary, particularly given how Helena had met the foreigner.

But she knew that he was now close to accepting the inevitable. He and his daughter had to flee Berlin and Germany, and Sam might be the key. Jacob had suffered on his visits to the police station. He would be made to sit for hours, until the desk sergeant became bored and told him to go home – reduced to the status of a humiliated dog. Even worse were the actions he witnessed against other Jewish people brought in for questioning. He resolved to bear witness to the maltreatment of his fellows.

In different times Sam would have been excited to have been invited to the grand house. Helena showed him into the hall, where he was impressed with the wide staircase and wooden panelling, the Chinese vases, the bronze bust, and the shiny coat-stand kept pristine with a flick of Erna's duster. As usual, the reminder of her tragic friend caused Helena a stab of grief. It seemed so long ago since she'd been killed. It had been weeks.

In the study, her father rose from his chair and offered Sam his hand, and the discussion began. The old man was impressed by his honesty as he explained his ignorance of the turmoil and persecution in the city, and told of his mission to assess the capability of the railways to assist in a war. He spoke so openly of Vernon Stainton, that Jacob cautioned him that in Berlin he must be more diplomatic.

After two hours, Sam knew exactly what he must do. He had to help Helena and her father gain British passports, and he must not lose contact with this woman he was falling in love with by the minute.

Helena felt it too, but she did not dare to show it. She was aware her emotional state was hardly normal, that death and persecution had permeated her life in every facet.

She was becoming more responsible for her father's well-being, also. They would be deserting their home and friends. They would be surviving from day to day rather than living a life that was once so comfortable.

It was hardly a good time to consider that she might be falling in love. But as much as she knew it to be irrational, it might just be inevitable.

Most of the time Vernon was an amiable drunk. Occasionally when he strayed from his favoured tipple of brandy he became unpredictable. It was late afternoon when he had fancied a change and reached for the bottle of gin. A G & T in the sunshine. Not too much tonic, plenty of ice. He left to sit outside.

An hour later he was feeling the effect. Not the warm glow of brandy and tranquillity with the world, but self-pity and the need to hurt. He felt the pressures piling on him. Willy was becoming a whingeing pain, Sam was tiresome and self-righteous and Herta was becoming stale and unattractive. How dare she discuss his personal business with the trainspotter? A wave of nostalgia swept over him as he yearned for his innocent childhood and doting mother. His English country garden, his nanny, Chocco his faithful labrador. He drained his glass and wiped a tear from his eye. It might as well have been pure gin; his body seemed full of it.

"You should see your face, Vernon." Herta said, as she cleared a table nearby. He was redder in the jowls than usual. "Wear a hat now that the sun is getting warmer by the day."

"Don't you tell me what to do, you fat German bitch," he spat at her.

At first, she thought it was just a jibe too far.

She could give as well as take when it came to harsh but jokey repartee, but this was different. Vernon's bloated face had somehow gained a hardness as his eyes had receded under heavy brows. He dribbled. She thought to ignore him and move on into the bar with the empty glasses and bottles she was carrying, but could not ignore his renewed attack.

"Whore! Did you tell the English spy my secrets as you lay beneath him?"

"Vernon. Look at you. Drunk and incapable, and you dare speak to me in such a way."

"I'll speak as I like. You work for me. Not that you show any gratitude or loyalty. What did you tell him?"

"I haven't told him anything. You don't know what you're talking about. Go to bed and sleep it off."

Vernon was enraged by her, and tried to stand up as she went inside carrying her empties, hurt by her lover's cruelty. But he was not done yet, and managed to extricate himself from his chair. He followed unsteadily into the bar. Regular customers were not overly surprised to see the fat Englishman lurch from side to side clumsily navigating his way around tables and chairs to the wide wooden bar where Herta stood washing glasses.

"Get me a large, a very large G & T, and no arguments," he demanded, attempting to hoist a buttock onto a barstool and failing miserably. "What are you looking at?"

Herta looked knowingly at him. "I see a dark dog day. Will you soon be crying for your momma's nipple?"

A regular bar drinker, a man in his late fifties, laughed loudly, which earned him a filthy look.

"Get out and don't come back!" Vernon shouted at him.

"Stay and ignore the old fool," Herta said contemptuously.

Vernon's blood almost burst through his temples and he lashed out at her, landing a clumsy roundhouse on her left cheek. And seconds later could not understand why he was on the bar room floor nursing a sore jaw, until a bleary-eyed version of Sam Bolton came into focus standing over him and comforting Herta. His befuddled brain slowly realised it had been rattled by the punch that felled his raddled body. He tried to get to his feet to extract revenge, but realising quickly he wouldn't make it to the vertical, rolled against the base of the bar and drifted.

It was a party. Screams and giggles. He had a sense of floating but not weightlessness, which was strange. Lights shone in his face but passed quickly. Whoops of delight as a door was pushed open.

Vernon wanted to sleep, not party. He wished the cacophony of noise would stop. Suddenly he was in bed. Soft warm comfort. But the noise, the cackling noise would not stop.

"Sure you're all right? Think you should see a doctor or somebody?" asked Sam. "No, it was a glancing blow." Herta handed him a glass of beer. The bar had quietened after the entertainment of the antics of the drunken Englishman. "He's always like this after gin."

"And how often's that?"

"Two or three times during the summer. Who knows what goes on in his head or what triggers it off? You acted very nobly."

Sam smiled.

"I didn't even think about it. If I'd have hit my boss back home in Doncaster I'd have been sacked immediately. I'm not quite sure what will happen now with Vernon."

"He'll do nothing against you. That I can assure."

Upstairs in his bedroom the 'party guest' was being stripped of his clothes by the transvestites. They had a great time at the expense of the drunken buffoon, and the squeals of delight at the discovery he wore sock suspenders could be heard down in the bar. Vernon wanted to leave and go to sleep. He was unaware he was in his own bed.

"Can they be trusted?" Sam asked. "The 'girls'."

"Definitely not," Herta said, and grinned. "It's

the first and last time he will ever hit me, though – they're my friends, not his. Vernon and Willy regard me as rather stupid but I am not. Because I don't talk above superficiality to them they also think I'm low. But I'm not. I'm saving, and one day I'll be moving to a better life."

There were more squeals of delight from upstairs. Sam tried not to wonder what was happening to Vernon.

SEVENTEEN

The bar was yet to open, but the cleaners had left everywhere in pristine condition, and the morning sunshine lit up the table where Vernon, Herta and Sam sat drinking their coffee. As a mark of his remorse, Vernon had foregone his usual brandy boost to start his day.

"If I need to apologise to more than you two then tell me and I'll do it. Gin's a family weakness and sometimes I forget that. I hope I can atone for my very bad behaviour."

"No need to worry on my part. If you are sincere," Herta said, surprising Sam by her casual tone.

"Of course I'm sincere. If nothing else I am an English gentleman. Sam, you won't be with us for much longer and I hope this won't be your lasting memory of me."

"Of course not, Vernon. Sometimes we all have a bit too much. It happened to me at our Gwen's wedding so I'm not one to judge. And I appreciate you saying you won't bear a grudge against me. I just arrived after you … well you and Herta. I didn't know how else to stop you … it was wrong of me."

"No, not at all. You were a knight in shining

armour. Can that be an end to it, then?"

"Definitely on my part," Sam said, and held out a conciliatory hand.

Vernon did the same. The men shook hands and Herta also smiled, before leaving to prepare the bar.

"What time is today's train, Sam?" Vernon asked, in what he considered an official tone.

"I'll leave in ten minutes," Sam said, and wondered how to introduce a more contentious subject. "But just before I go …"

"The passport and papers for your Jewish friends?" Vernon anticipated. He looked his most approachable. Sam thought he must be genuinely contrite about the night before.

"Yes," he said. "If it's—"

"I'll speak to Willy later," Vernon said. "I'm sure that it can all be arranged." Sam was delighted.

"They…" he started, "… and I … we would be ever so grateful, Vernon. Thanks."

Later that day, despite a monumental hangover, Vernon travelled across the city to meet Willy in a bar. He did not beat about the bush.

"Bloody Yorkshire oik," he spat. "Lauding it over me with his high morals. He hasn't a clue about anything."

"What exactly has happened?" Willy asked. "You look particularly awful today. Has your guest upset you so much?"

"I'll tell you what, my Fatherland-loving friend, he's crystallised a plan for me that I've been formulating in my mind since we last spoke. I know how to solve all our current problems. All of them."

Vernon drained his glass of brandy. He was back on track.

"The twins?" said Diefenbaker, hopefully. "You know how to get rid of them?"

"Oh yes, the whole damned bloody lot. Herta too, if she doesn't shape up. How dare these patronising plebians think they can treat me with such disdain? With my background. My connections. How bloody dare they?"

"The twins, though, Vernon. What's going to happen?"

"They'll no longer be your stuff of nightmares, Willy. For a start-off, you need to arm the idiots. That won't be a problem, will it?"

"Arm them?" To Willy's mind it was ridiculous. The problem was that they could kill so easily already. "Are you seriously suggesting we give them guns?"

"You haven't heard me yet. And it's just a Luger apiece I'm talking about. A Luger and plenty of ammo. Listen."

At first Diefenbaker thought the plan sounded fanciful, then on reflection, that it was brilliant. He had to thank his English friend and colleague, he said, most sincerely. It meant that they would each rid themselves of terrible nuisances.

And be allowed to carry on their lucrative business as before.

When Sam handed the travel documents to Helena she seemed to grow in stature. Her smile was the sweetest thing he had ever seen, and she spontaneously hugged and kissed him on the cheek. He held on to her and they looked into each other's eyes. Mutually, without words or change of expression, they came to the same conclusion.

The next kiss was not out of gratitude. She was beautiful, and her lips on his were the best sensation of his life. He never wanted it to end but of course it must, and they looked again into each other's eyes, and this time it was different.

Despite himself Sam thought of Gwen and her telling him that he would know the right one when she came along. Dare he hope she had? Helena, aware her father was close by in his study, took Sam's hand, and her smile seemed to levitate him. He hardly knew her but he never wanted to be apart from her again.

Jacob Rosenhoff fought back the tears as he handled his new British passport. His feelings were so mixed he could hardly focus enough to thank the young man standing with his daughter. The papers, with the stamp, the signature, the authority were worth more than a fortune: they were the key to escaping from the nightmare. They could travel to France. He could help prevent what seemed to be an impending disaster.

Jacob got up from his chair and hugged Helena. After a few moments she included Sam, and it was the first indication to her father that the Englishman meant perhaps more to her than just the provider of their salvation.

Much more.

"So, they were pleased?" asked Vernon, sitting back and waiting for the wave of gratitude to engulf him.

"You have saved their lives, Vernon. Theirs and maybe many more. Pleased is very much an understatement," Sam said.

Herta delivered two steins of beer. A rare drink for Vernon, but he had pledged to moderate his daytime drinking, and considered beer just a cut above water.

Sam sipped his drink, satisfied that all was fine. His reports had been well received back home and he believed that he'd even helped Vernon become a better man. Also, he was on the verge of falling in love, and thought that Helena felt the same. He'd miss her terribly when she left for France with her father, but they had vowed to find each again and nothing would stop them being together in the future. He knew his mother would take to her immediately, as would Gwen and Edith, and if Dad had reservations about her being foreign, her masterly English would help to win him over.

He didn't know where the Rosenhoffs would base themselves after the French visit, and thought London was probably best. They could not return to Berlin for the foreseeable future, and Doncaster didn't seem the right place at all.

"I've made a few enquiries about the Évian Conference," Vernon said seriously. "I think you should accompany your Jewish friends."

It came out of the blue for Sam, who had to smile.

"Do you think so? I'm not sure if it would be allowed."

"Allowed by whom? I'm your Berlin handler." Vernon leaned forward conspiratorially. "It would be at my discretion, and London would accept that without question. The conference is vitally important and your presence would help to get them there. Then from France you could travel home. Your time here's almost up anyway."

Sam could barely contain himself.

"I must say that I hadn't thought of that," he said, "but it's a great idea. Thanks, Vernon. If you think it would be all right I'd be delighted."

"Good. So you see, old Vernon's come through for you after all."

"Yes, you have. Vernon, thank you."

EIGHTEEN

The Lugers had been easy to obtain and cheaper than Willy had imagined. Ammunition was plentiful and just as simple. He'd taken the twins to some woods not too far away where they could practise, and he had to admit that they were both good shots. They'd grown up firing shotguns from an early age but not pistols, but their hands were steady and their eyes good; they would be very efficient gunmen and killers.

Passports and travel documents were issued along with German marks and English pounds, and Max and Bruno could hardly wait to start out on their mission. They already envisaged their triumphant return to their homeland, where they would be greeted as heroes. Willy, also, could not wait to be rid of them. Vernon was very confident that both men would either be killed or incarcerated. Willy preferred the former.

Helena's emotions were in turmoil. She was still grieving for Erna, and the death of her servant friend had also stirred up memories of her mother, causing immense sadness at her double loss. This was mixed in with the upheaval of leaving home, probably forever, and the uncertainty of a new life who knew where. If all this were not enough, what was she to make of Sam? What did she truly feel about him? If they had met under different circumstances, would she have given him a second glance? She needed him for survival, but how had that affected her feelings towards him?

It was almost all too much to bear; too much to take into consideration. She decided to concentrate on making sure her father arrived safely in France. The future would have to wait.

Sam had also not slept well. He had called to see Helena and her father to suggest travelling with them to Évian, and been delighted with their response. Jacob had warmed to the young Englishman and accepted the idea readily. Although both he and his daughter spoke optimistically about returning when their nightmare was over, each feared that it would never happen. They had to resign themselves to lives lived in exile from their homeland.

There would be many priceless memories left behind along with family treasures, but some they could quickly convert to cash. It would be a fraction of the true value, but with the risk of attracting unwanted attention it had to be done. Jacob had only one man he could trust: a faithful employee – and a gentile – from the days when the furniture factory was well run, profitable and a cohesive unit within the local community. Jacob would entrust him with keys to the house, and instructions how to dispose of the contents, depending on circumstances.

Sam had naturally discussed his plans with Vernon at some length. He would leave the bar mid-morning for the Rosenhoff's house, then the three of them would travel to Potsdamer Bahnhof and take a train to Paris, then on to Évian, a journey of about nine hours. Jacob had many contacts waiting for him, and three days to prepare before addressing the conference that he hoped would change many lives.

When Sam did drop off, his sleep was disturbed by unsettling dreams. He had packed his belongings and his departure would be leisurely, but he found it hard to relax. There was a small alarm clock in the room which was disturbing him, and he resolved to give it five more minutes, then pack it away if he was still awake. He had no fear of oversleeping.

As the final minute came he heard his bedroom door slowly opening, and saw the silhouette of a woman in a dressing gown framed in the doorway. Sam realised that it was Herta, and felt strangely excited – and confused. He'd found her attractive from the moment he'd first seen her, but there was Helena now. He also knew for Vernon's mistress to be in his room in the middle of the night was unlikely to be straightforward, however naturally his young man's instincts were urging him to fling back the sheets and invite her in.

Herta jerked the gown closer to her, and gestured unromantically for him to be silent. She sat on his bed and said quietly, "All is not good. I know Vernon is not a man of honour, but he has done a terrible thing, even for him."

Sam was puzzled. Vernon had done good things of late, very good. He'd sold the passports and travel documents at a reasonable price; he'd suggested Sam travel with Helena and her father; he'd even boosted his funds for the journey out of his own pocket. What could Herta be talking about? His expression asked the question.

"I decoded a message that he's sent to London," she said. "I had my suspicions. I know him only too well."

"A message?"

"He has said that you're absconding with a lot of money. He says although he's helped you write your reports, your work has been lazy and shoddy because you've fallen for a Jewish woman. Who has got you underneath her spell."

Sam, wide awake, was now bolt upright.

"We'll see about that," he said. He'd confront Stainton immediately. But Herta stopped him.

"No," she said, urgently. "He will have you

arrested. You must be cleverer than that."

"And do what?"

"I'll tell you all I know before you decide. Willy has sent the two brothers, the idiot twins, to England on a mission. He thought I'd be impressed, because it's to sabotage some speed record. He thinks it's important for the Reich."

"What record?" asked Sam Bolton. Although he knew. Oh yes, damn well he knew! "It's a record held by the Fatherland. Diefenbaker was very enthusiastic that it must stay in our country. Britain must not take it."

"Herta, what is all this about? First of all, am I really likely to be arrested?"

"Yes, you are. And that's why you must be clever. I know about the Jews and how you wish to help them, and you have my sympathy. My advice is not to travel your planned route. Vernon knows all your details. You will not get to France."

"I can change our travel plans, I'm sure I can," said Sam. "But is Vernon really such a lowlife he'd betray and lie like this?"

She nodded, sombrely.

"Yes, Sam Bolton. He thinks only of himself, and you have threatened his cosy existence. You've also offended his stupid honour greatly, and he is vindictive."

It took Sam a little while to accept the enormity

of what Herta had told him. Such despicable action was beyond his experience, and almost his belief, but he had to accept it as the truth. "All right," he said, at last. "I believe you unconditionally. About Willy. And the twins going to England. But the mission? Exactly what's that meant to be?"

"Willy wanted to impress me with his power," Herta said calmly. "He wants me in his bed, and I can tell you it will not happen. He tells me many things which I pretend to be interested in, he cannot help himself. The twins have been sent to England to kill somebody. Somebody I have heard you talk about."

"Who?"

"Grisely? Grossley? Something like that."

It hit Sam like a locomotive.

"Oh my God," he said. "Gresley. They're going to kill Sir Nigel Gresley!"

NINETEEN

Max and Bruno Shafer were already on their way. As their German locomotive thundered along the metals, they felt great pride that they were serving the Fatherland at last. They had been given great powers by Herr Diefenbaker, who had told them that High Command itself was monitoring their progress and that a special assignment awaited them.

England had the audacity to be attempting to take the speed record from their own *Fliegender Hamburger*, they'd been told, and usurp it with a steam engine called *Mallard*. This attempt would take place on July 3rd and it was up to them to stop it by killing the Chief Engineer of the project, Sir Nigel Gresley. They already had a Luger each, and glory would be theirs.

If they should be captured, Herr Diefenbaker had assured them, they would not be shot as spies, but would be handed over to the German Embassy in London and repatriated, as was diplomatic law. On their return home, he would not be surprised if the Führer himself was not there to greet them! The two returning heroes would be commissioned in the army. As officers. Obvious.

Hook, line and sinker, the two idiots fell for it.

Breakfast was a strain for Sam, torture. He ate sparingly sitting across from Vernon, who was up and functioning uncharacteristically early. Herta served them, acting as if her visit to Sam in the night had indeed been a dream. He wished it had, but sadly not. He had been betrayed and now Sir Harry Trafford and even the man he must save, Sir Nigel Gresley, might think him a thief. His instinct was to confront Vernon, have it out with him man to man but he heeded Herta's warnings. He must swallow personal injustices and think of the more important issues. He must avoid arrest, help get the Rosenhoffs to safety, and alert the authorities in England to Gresley's mortal danger.

He thought how his family would be most upset if the police visited, accusing him of all sorts of fictitious crimes. Mam and dad would not believe it of course, but dad would undoubtedly blame foreigners, saying nothing good would ever come from a trip abroad. Gwen and Edith would be upset, and he imagined Edgar offering to fight anyone who thought that there might be an ounce of truth in the allegations.

As Vernon waffled on hypocritically about the valuable contribution Sam had made to England's security, Sam thought about his plan. He would convince the Rosenhoffs to accompany him to England, not France. They could travel there afterwards for the conference as there was ample time. In England he'd phone Norman, who he'd got on so well with on their car trip from London to the coast, but if he failed to convince him he was telling the truth he wasn't sure what he would do next. The speed record attempt was in two days' time. He would have to be there.

Leaving the bar for the last time, Sam could see the relief on Vernon's bloated, ruddy face. He had to bite his tongue hard as the two men parted on the pretence of good terms. Herta too wished him well, but she was sincere. After their last farewells Sam, suitcase in hand, boarded a tram for the Rosenhoffs.

Jacob and Helena had expected to leave for France not England as Sam was now suggesting. Worn down by grief, humiliation and disappointment, their senses were on heightened alert for treachery, and what Sam told them made little sense. Why would Vernon supply the travel documents only to betray them? They had no intention to do him harm, and would be forever grateful to their saviour. Why would his mistress visit Sam in the night and betray her lover, her employer, her security?

No, none of it made sense, and they were reluctant

to reconsider the original escape plan. It seemed so unnecessary for them to go to England. Who was this Sir Nigel Gresley that Sam seemed to care so much about?

Sam fought to keep calm. He knew that every minute was now precious. He had examined his options and knew that he had to get out of Germany as quickly as possible, as he could be arrested on Vernon and Willy's say so. He could be lost in a nightmare judicial system that could lock him away for God knows how long. He had to return immediately to England. He had to make Jacob and Helena see that he was only wanting to do the right thing.

Vernon and Willy had forgotten the original joke. The one that had led them into paroxysms of uncontrollable laughter. Immediate worries over, they had drunk almost a bottle of brandy and many glasses of beer, two affable middle-aged men over-indulging and enjoying each other's company. How could other customers know that between them they had sent two insane killers on a suicidal attempted assassination, and blackened a totally innocent man's character, all for their own self-preservation?

Herta watched, loathing them more and more by the minute, knowing it was time for her to move on. She had liked Sam not out of lust, but because he was a man of principle. He was of good character and one day would be a sound and reliable husband. She had not spoken to Helena, but had seen her a few times and suspected they were in love. She wished them well, regretted that her life was unfulfilled, and sympathised with their efforts to escape.

Despising the two drunks made Herta despise herself and how she had been the English 'gentleman's' lover. She shuddered at the thought of how he could have been so callous as to make false accusations to quash any threat to his dissolute lifestyle. The 'girls', who knew lots of other people in lots of other bars, had often said that she could do better for herself. And now they would help her find another job – she was leaving the next morning.

Vernon Stainton shouted for more drinks and Herta obliged him. In her own time.

Sam's frustration had been growing by the minute. Following Vernon's betrayal, he thought the authorities might be at the Rosenhoff's door at any time to pick them up for obtaining false documents, and he was also now wanted for theft. Eventually, after a lot of persuasion, Helena and Jacob agreed to accompany Sam to England, and he was giddy with relief. Reasoning they would be looked for on the Berlin-Paris train, he had worked out an alternative route from his experiences of studying rail traffic.

They would travel slightly circuitously to Zeebrugge, and cross to England that night. He would then telephone Norman Rigby and explain everything. He felt confident all would be well.

London was experiencing a lovely spring morning as Norman sat in his Ministry of Transport office in Curzon Street. He was concentrating on a report concerning the number of mess-kit holders purchased by the German army, which could help him estimate troop numbers nearly as accurately as rifles manufactured, a secret of the German State. When he was interrupted by Sir Harry Trafford, he folded his report and gave full attention to his boss.

"That chap, Sam Bolton, you drove him down for the cross-Channel ferry a few weeks ago. Yorkshire through and through, seemed a decent sort to me."

"Me too," said Norman. "Is anything wrong sir?"

"Plenty I'm afraid. He's absconded with the Berlin petty cash – actually, not so petty. I must be slipping. I had him down as a salt-of-the-earth man. How about you?"

"Obviously didn't get to know him that well given the time restraint, but I also thought he was a good sort. Bit of a shock, sir."

"More to come. There's a chance that he might be

a murderer."

"What? Surely not, sir! What's happened?"

Sir Harry blew air out through his lips.

"Vernon Stainton's been found dead in bed. It may be natural causes, but it's a pretty stiff coincidence. A scant few hours after he reports the loss of a substantial amount of money and an operative missing, he's found stone dead. I have people looking into it, but Bolton must be located as quickly as possible."

"And where do we start?"

"As far as we know he's heading for Paris with his Jewish girlfriend and her father. The Germans are on the lookout for the three of them. Damned awkward business all round."

The train was crowded with people heading for work or celebrations in Wolfsburg. The old city had been modernised and industrialised beyond recognition and as new buildings and amenities came on stream bands played and communities partied. Sam knew he and the Rosenhoff's could travel there with confidence of being engulfed by the crowds, and they'd decided to sit in separate seats to avoid being an obvious trio.

The arrangement seemed to have worked as they were ignored by fellow travellers, except for one man who took a shine to Helena after sitting opposite. But she remained polite and cool, and soon he accepted his pursuit was pointless. He concentrated on his newspaper after that and Helena and Sam relaxed. Jacob remained blissfully ignorant of the whole affair.

Vernon looked fitter and healthier lying dead in the mortuary than he ever had in life. This is true of many corpses after the undertaker's cosmetics have been applied, but this was before. It was as if his body, relieved of commands from a hedonistic brain, could now relax and be itself.

Herta viewed her ex-lover with many emotions. As well as being hedonistic, he'd been vain, greedy, lazy, vindictive – but occasionally kind. She would try and remember those rare occasions, along with his maudlin and child-like reminiscences of his early life in England, his meanderings about nannies, labradors, school japes and long warm summers. Willy had offered to oversee the funeral arrangements, and Herta was happy with that. She would draw a line under that chapter of her life, and move on.

Preliminary medical speculation was of a heart attack, unsurprising given Vernon's lifestyle, but a post-mortem would follow. The cost of repatriating the body to England led Willy and Herta to discuss money. He had access to the 'float' cash used in the passport and travel document business, but wondered where Vernon's personal fortune was kept.

"We can expect a visit from his government, I

think," Herta suggested. A couple of Englishmen called in to the bar occasionally, and although Vernon had never confirmed it, she suspected they were British agents.

Willy agreed.

"They will want to know the cause of death, although I'd say that is obvious and unquestionable. The business is another matter. And I've no idea what they might know about me."

"And your instructions to the twins despatched to England?" Herta said, provocatively.

Willy bristled at her impertinence, but he restrained his feelings. He needed her to access Vernon's cash.

"It's a time for great discretion, Herta. It's time for Germans such as us to put the Fatherland, and our personal loyalties, first."

TWENTY

In her street in Doncaster, Sam Bolton's mother paled at the sight of the policeman on her doorstep. Her first thoughts were that her mother must have died or that there had been an accident at The Plant involving her husband or Edgar. When invited inside, hopefully before being seen by any neighbours, the bobby soon dismissed those fears.

And when she heard the purpose of the visit she burst out laughing out of sheer relief. Sam a thief linked to a mysterious death, it was ridiculous! Her Sam on the run, heading for France with a couple that he hardly knew; it was nonsensical!

She offered the officer a cup of tea while they sorted the misunderstanding out.

Herta and Willy were in the cellar of the bar. He was almost shaking with anticipation as she produced the key to a massive old safe. She had told him that Vernon had been the only person to use it and she had no idea what it contained.

Willy took control. The key turned with a satisfying clunk as the mechanism drew back the bolts, and he was surprised at the weight of the door as he pulled it open so he and Herta could look inside.

The contents were surprisingly well ordered. Folders and files containing orders and bills, invoices paid and outstanding. There was also a large number of blank British passports, and a disappointingly small amount of cash. Diefenbaker speculated that the British agents who called at the bar had left with money to fund their activities in Germany.

Herta knew better. And she kept it to herself.

Sam and the Rosenhoffs, having travelled through Hanover and Osnabruck, arrived at Zeebrugge in time for the boat to England. After the ferry had cast off their confidence grew, and they spoke openly to each other as they felt the sea beneath them and the Belgian coast receded. It was Friday, the 1st of July – two days before the record attempt, and five before the start of the conference at Évian.

Sam had almost firmed up a plan. His first priority was making sure Helena and Jacob would be safe and free to travel when the time came. They had money, but they would be strangers in England, and he did not want them risking their freedom by associating with him until he had cleared up the problems caused by Vernon. But he felt confident Norman and Sir Harry Trafford would believe his story, and his information about the imminent threat to Sir Nigel's life. He had thought it all through.

He had also found out that there was a strong Jewish community in the East End of London, and he had the address of a family who would hopefully remember him as the man who helped them at the underground. He would direct Helena and her father to them, confident that they would sympathise with Jacob's mission. And after that, when he'd been found innocent of all charges, he would either travel with them or reunite on their return from France. After that he just wanted to spend as much time as possible with Helena.

He would also phone Edgar at their social club the following evening. Saturday was snooker night, and Edgar, being a creature of habit, would certainly be playing. He would tell his brother-in-law everything and have him reassure the family. Sam was optimistic that all would turn out well in the end.

Bruno and Max sat next to each other on the train journey to Liverpool Street station. They took up three seats sitting impassively facing four more people occupying the coach. No-one spoke. One of the English passengers had tried to engage the twins in conversation but had been stone-walled. Willy had advised them not to speak unless it was absolutely necessary and as their knowledge of the English language was nil they found comfort in silence.

Willy had kept their mission instructions stark and simple. With knowledge passed on from Vernon he told them to travel to Grantham on the morning of Sunday the 3rd of July, and kill Sir Nigel Gresley. He didn't give them the faintest chance of succeeding, but the point was to have them locked up abroad, or killed. Either way he would be rid of them, and if they did manage to disrupt the record attempt by *Mallard*, then that would be a bonus.

The Channel crossing was smooth and without incident. Jacob wrote letters and rested, while Sam and Helena spent time finding out more about each other. Family histories revealed little in common, but they did not care. They were together and that was all that mattered.

After disembarking at Harwich, they had lunch in a café overlooking the sea where they took stock and planned ahead. Helena and Jacob agreed that the Jewish community in the East End was a place of sanctuary, and because their English was good and they had the wherewithal for their journey they agreed to travel without Sam. He would head for Grantham and alert everybody about the danger to Sir Nigel's life.

Sam assured the Rosenhoffs that all would be well after his explanations. He hoped to accompany them to Évian and help enlighten others as he had been himself about the Jewish plight. They said their farewells at the station and Jacob turned away discreetly as his daughter and Sam kissed goodbye. It was a lovers' kiss. They would meet again in two or three days' time.

Sam found a public phone box and rang Norman on his home number. Before he could fully explain his story, he was horrified to find out that Vernon Stainton was dead.

"I didn't steal any money," he insisted. "And Vernon was certainly alive when I left."

Norman was guarded.

"It seems probable that it was a heart attack but we can't be sure yet. He died just as you left, Sam."

"Herta will vouch for me. She's his barmaid. And his mistress"

"That's what Uncle Harry was hoping for, but she's gone missing. Our people in Berlin can't find her, so it's a long shot," Norman said.

"I know it all seems far-fetched," Sam said, "but it is the truth. This is so important."

"All right, Sam. But an operative in Berlin is dead and a considerable amount of money has been stolen. He reported you for the theft. You need to give yourself up and explain everything."

It was the last thing Sam was going to do. He

imagined himself locked away while Sir Nigel's life was threatened and the Rosenhoffs perhaps stranded in Britain.

"Norman, please, listen to me. Four weeks ago, I knew nothing. My head was full of cricket, football, my job and how I was going to get on. I knew nothing of anything that wasn't about me."

"We've heard you've fallen for a girl, and she has you under her spell," Norman said. As if offering an explanation for any irrationality.

"That might be true, but … no, Norman, there's more, much, much more. A massive group of people is being persecuted by another mass of people and it's not right. It's far from right, but now I can do something about it. The first thing is to convince you to convince others, until enough people are convinced to make a massive difference. It's our duty to stop this madness."

Norman hesitated.

"But there are limits to my job, Sam." He had sympathy with Sam's statement, but saw it as an internal German matter.

"No," Sam said. "We're not talking limits. As far as I can see, your job is to help keep Britain safe, and that doesn't mean pulling the drawbridge up. It doesn't stop at the border. A man keeps his own family safe by looking after everybody else's. Jacob Rosenhoff told me that, and he desperately needs to get to the Évian conference to tell it to the world. When people know, especially in our country, refugees, starting with innocent children, will be welcomed and taken care of here. We have to do it, Norman. Or we're no better than those monsters persecuting them."

Sam explained everything else he knew, and his passion impressed Norman.

But Norman was a realist. "It's how it looks to the police and the department," he reasoned. "There's money missing, and an unexplained death. Those twin assassins could be considered a red herring. A fantasy."

"Norman, the threat to Sir Nigel Gresley's life is real. There are two maniacs out to kill him, no matter what anybody thinks about me. That is a fact. He has to be protected. Can you contact Harry Trafford?"

"It's the weekend, and I've no idea where he is," said Norman. "Even if I did speak to him I know he'd just want you arrested and brought in for questioning."

"But I've got to make sure the Rosenhoffs get to France. And first, I have to go to Grantham to warn everybody."

"The police may well pick you up," said Norman. "It'll be much worse if you're on the run. Give yourself up, and tell them everything you've just told me."

Sam knew he had to have help, and the only way he could get it was by trusting Norman.

"All right," he said, reluctantly. "I will. But only to you. And only on the understanding that you'll drive me up to Grantham as soon as possible."

He was putting all his trust in someone that he barely knew.

"This is so important, Norman," he said. "So important."

TWENTY ONE

Apart from Norman, reasoned Sam when the call was over, no one knew he was in England. The authorities might be looking for him in Germany or France – almost certainly were – but the chances of being arrested by a bobby on the beat in Harwich were pretty slim.

Even so he would have to be extremely cautious, because so much depended on him reaching Grantham in one piece. They had arranged to meet close to where Norman had dropped him off almost four weeks before, but he could not get there until the early hours of Sunday morning, however hard he drove. After that the one hundred and fifty or so miles from Harwich to Grantham would take perhaps four hours, which meant the time they had to catch the *Mallard* run would be cut very fine. It was set to start around eleven in the morning.

After making his arrangement with Norman, there was nothing Sam could do but wait. Hunger got the better of him and he returned to the café he'd visited earlier. After eating, as inconspicuously as possible, he returned to the phone box and located Edgar in the Railway Club.

"Edgar, this is so important – it's a matter of

life and death. You've got to warn HNG his life's in danger."

He was speaking as clearly and as loudly as he dared, but the background of the club's Saturday night drinkers and a crackling line did not help.

"Sam," said Edgar, "you know the police called at your house, don't you?"

"That doesn't matter, Edgar. Not for now."

"It mattered to your mam, lad; she was mortified. So when can you come home and sort it out? Everything!"

"I'm on my way, but listen to what I'm telling you! Hello … Hello Edgar? Are you still there?"

"Sam, it's a bloody awful …"

"Edgar. If you can hear me. Two German men, they look like prop forwards. They're going to try and kill HNG tomorrow … hello … Edgar … hello."

Sam put the receiver down in frustration. He knew he was wasting his time, as the club phone had never been reliable. Few people ever used it, so the committee didn't care …

It was the early hours of the morning in King's Cross depot when the fire was lit. *Mallard* would be warmed up slowly, ensuring the boiler and components were heated uniformly. Risk of leaks were kept to a minimum if all the metal expanded at the same rate. The precision-made machine was only recently run-in, and needed gentle handling by experienced men. Increasing warmth would coax the gentle beast to life.

In the port where Sam was lurking, there were comings and goings all night long: wagons arriving and leaving; a crew waiting for their berths. As dawn broke early steamer passengers arrived, and Sam kept well out of the way. He had slept fitfully on a bench overlooking the sea, but now he was on the lookout for Norman.

Mallard's tender, full of coal and water, was attached, while the fire grew under tight control. As the heat increased, the boiler pressure gauge needle rose from zero, and climbed steadily and slowly. Full pressure of 250psi was still hours away, as bearings, connecting rods and all metal moving parts were soaked in lubricants.

An aniseed-oil stink bomb was fitted to the middle cylinder big end. If the bearing overheated, as it had done in the past, it would activate the bomb.

Sam stretched his legs. It was a lovely early summer's morning. The sun shone, the seagulls spiralled and the air was fresh. He would have enjoyed himself if it were not for the responsibility heavy on his shoulders, and he went to eat breakfast in preparation for the day ahead.

By now he was scruffy and unshaven, but his

appearance was the least of his worries, even when Norman, who'd had a good night's sleep, drove up looking refreshed and smartly groomed. They set off with the car top down, and the flying breeze helped him tell his story, which shocked Norman although he believed it now in every last detail.

Vernon Stainton's behaviour was bordering on treason, they agreed, and he'd escaped scot free by dying! The murderous twins Norman found fascinating, and their appalling mission spurred him on. He drove the car 'like a bat out of hell' through the empty Essex countryside towards Grantham, Lincolnshire.

They knew that it was touch and go. *Mallard* was due to turn around at Barkston and they had to be there. If they missed their chance, then everything was lost.

Including Sir Nigel Gresley's life. For Sam worked out it was at this point that the assassination attempt had to take place.

They had to be there.

TWENTY TWO

Mallard had six coaches. They were Silver Jubilee Coronation class, and between them and the tender was a special car – a dynamometer car – built in an age of Georgian elegance, all shining brass and polished wood. It had comfortable chairs and a sturdy table, which supported an array of fine and beautiful recording instruments.

With rolls of paper and ink pens attached to mark its speed over every yard it steamed, the train was ready to undertake the record run. Now all it lacked was crew and passengers. And they had started to arrive.

The early morning sunshine highlighted the garter blue livery of the barely four-month-old locomotive hissing in the traps, conserving her tons of coal and water in the tender. Economy was the key. Nothing wasted. Every ounce of energy utilised to the full. Coal to heat the water, water converted to steam to power the pistons. Massive six-foot eight-inch driving wheels perfectly balanced to turn half way round with every piston stroke.

Driver Joseph Duddington, Fireman Thomas Bray, and Supervisor Inspector Sid Jenkins climbed aboard the footplate. Railwaymen through and through, they made their inspections. She was heating nicely. On schedule as planned.

The others arrived. Westinghouse people, whose founder George had invented the air brake in the last century. Sir Nigel greeted them and they wondered about the dynamometer car. Informed about the record attempt on the return run after the brake testing, they were offered taxis instead of taking the high-speed risk. All declined. They wouldn't miss the attempt for anything.

Fired up, *Mallard* – seventy feet long, weighing over 165 tons – had stopped three times carrying out brake trials. She was now corralled at Barkston, before the run south. In the dynamometer car, the excitement grew as engineers and assistants checked the delicate monitoring machines. Paper rolls must not jam, a stylo must not run out of ink. Sir Nigel was quietly confident among his loyal crew.

Driver Duddington was waiting for instructions, raring to go. A man known for his skill and bravery, if anyone could achieve this for *Mallard* it was he, with his regular fireman Tommy Bray. Reliable and experienced, with an instinctive knowledge of its needs, they were both in tune with the engine, its sounds, its smells.

The fire was right, the boiler pressure up to 250psi

and the water level correct.

Max and Bruno Shafer had arrived the night before, and camped out as they had been used to all their lives. Friendly locals had assisted the 'German Hikers' as the English do, with faint amusement at their lack of the native language. They had guided them right to the railway line, assuming them to be trainspotters.

Driver Duddington and Tommy Bray had been chosen because they had the nerve to take the beast over the 90mph recommended limit for this track. No fools, they knew what could and could not be done, not reckless tyros but men with physical and mental strength. On the footplate, all hearts were racing in anticipation of the task ahead. Duddington turned his cap backwards and looked to Inspector Jenkins standing out of the way at the rear. When he nodded his approval, Duddington winked at Bray. The race was on.

    Slowly, Duddington squeezed the release handle on top of the reverser lever and pushed it forward. He turned the cylinder drain cock valve and blew the whistle. The sound was loud and strong. On footplate and in dynamometer car behind, confidence abounded.

    Sam and Norman heard the whistle, and the railwayman feared he knew the reason it was blown

– the attempt was beginning. As the sports car swept round a bend to reveal the straight road running close beside the railway track, Sam also saw two burly men climb surreptitiously aboard the last carriage as the train gained traction and momentum.

"The twins!" he shouted. And Norman nodded. The massive, evil twins from Germany.

Duddington had released the brake and opened the throttle, and Sam urged Norman to speed up too. Which he did.

"You won't make it on board though, Sam," he said. "You can't. Impossible."

"I've got to. She'll pass through Grantham station at no more than 24 mph. Get me close and I'll get aboard then. After that, we'll run out of road."

Norman did the best he could. He steered as close as he dared to, until the noise from the steel wheels was louder than his own engine. They could smell *Mallard*'s smoke, and it occasionally smothered them. It was black, but would soon be light grey when Fireman Bray had all in balance.

Closer yet, the carriage dwarfed the little car. Sam stood, braced himself, and leaned outwards. But as he touched the carriage, the sports car drifted right.

The second attempt was better. Up ahead, Sam could see that the road veered to the right and the rail track to the left – it was now or never. Grabbing with both hands, he left the car and hung on to the carriage, with the tarmac racing past beneath his feet. As Norman followed the road, *Mallard* surged off to the left and Sam climbed up to the roof.

And clung.

Inside their own carriage, their piggy eyes rounded with amazement, Bruno and Max watched it all. Recognised Sam and fumbled for their automatic pistols.

Far ahead, Driver Duddington accelerated to 60 mph, and the dynamometer engineers concentrated on their instruments. Sam crawled forward on top of the rear coach, knowing he had to reach the locomotive cab and warn them of the danger.

Somewhere below him, Max and Bruno were confused. They took their Lugers from their waistbands and moved forward in the empty carriage. They would progress from coach to coach and shoot anyone who tried to stop them. But the door was locked. There was no way through.

The men in the dynamometer car saw their speed registering 69 mph, and watched it increase to 74 as they topped Stoke Bank. Fireman Bray, well in his stride, was maintaining a rhythm of about six shovels of coal into the firebox every two minutes or so. The smokestack issue was now light grey: good fire.

But Sam's progress was too slow. He had to stand on the carriages and jump between them, and although his balance was good, the wind he fought against was getting ever stronger. Vague memories of Western films, with gallant cowboys racing over lumbering trucks with enormous six-shooters at the ready, became ridiculous – he doubted those old wood-burners had been doing more than thirty miles an hour! And he realised with horror the daily risks brakemen had taken every day turning roof-top wheels to apply brakes manually before Westinghouse had invented his revolutionary vacuum system.

Then suddenly, a new horror gripped him. Max and Bruno – two evil bullet heads – were at the rear of his coach, and struggling to clamber onto the roof. Almost blindly, he jumped on to the fifth carriage, and fought to get his balance back. Then, reckless with desperation, he increased his pace to almost reach the fourth.

The twins, though much less steady, were frighteningly brave. They watched him as he contemplated the yawning, swaying, gap, and they seemed almost calm. And then Max Schafer stopped, and released the safety catch of his pistol. He was frightening. He was like a rock.

On the last of the Coronation Coaches, Sam was almost at the dynamometer car. After that it was the tender, which he could move across to reach the footplate and the men he had to warn. While beneath them, indifferent, *Mallard* sped on at an ever-better pace.

Sir Nigel and the engineers, tense and silent, watched the dynamometer pens recording the miles per hour: 104 … 107 … 111½ … 116 … 119. Above them Sam Bolton leaned into the wind and struggled on. Until suddenly, a searing pain bit into him and he was on his knees. Instinctively he grabbed his thigh, and his hand was covered in hot, red blood. Behind him, Max Schafer prepared a second shot. The Englishman would die.

This time the tearing gale was Sam's best friend. As *Mallard* careered on, a good aim was impossible. The movement was gigantic, the howling wind beyond resistance, the Luger swinging uncontrollably. Max dropped to his knees to move forward while his brother stuck his gun back in his waistband to use both hands. And Sam crawled on.

Beneath the struggle, completely unaware, Sir Nigel and his team were engrossed with their machines: 120¾ … 122½ … 123 mph.

As Max appeared above him on the dynamometer car and took aim again, Sam dropped to the tender. The Luger was rock-steady now, but Sam had one chance left, one weapon of his own. Teeth gritted against the pain, he selected a piece of coal about the size of a cricket ball. With the accuracy of a return from mid-on to Edgar keeping wicket, he hit Max right between the eyes.

The old against the new. English coal against foreign technology. And coal, again, was king …

As the Nazi killer rolled off the train, its speed was recorded at 124mph. Sam turned to crawl across the coals to safety, but felt the pain in his leg increase as Bruno pulled him back. With nothing to grip on but loose coal, they both slipped between the tender and the recording car. Beneath was certain death. For both of them.

In the next seconds, at milepost 90¼, *Mallard* travelled at 124¼ mph, and finally 125 – and Sam realised with a shock what had stopped him from falling to the track. It was the platform Edgar had fitted up for him – the crazy, dangerous, platform, completely lethal at this speed. But if he could hang on to it, he might still live. His brother-in-law might even save his life …

The noise was tremendous, steel thundering on steel. A foot, a hand, a limb would be severed instantly, or a whole body cut in half under relentless, massive wheels. Sam clung on. The wind screamed, the oil spat, near boiling water splashed. The smells he'd always loved – of steam, hot oil, soot, grease, coal – were forced unpleasantly into his nostrils as the machine powered through the chaos. His arms ached but he had to hold on. A second's relaxation of a muscle, a loss of concentration, would surely mean death. But that was not all. A man, hell-bent on killing him, was also desperately clamped onto the platform.

The last surviving Schafer twin was immensely strong. Despite all the forces fighting him he reached to pull the gun out of his waistband. Sam, gripping tight with his left hand, grabbed his wrist with his right but Bruno, slowly and surely, forced the Luger towards his face. With muscles burning, Sam gripped *Mallard*'s tender and the wrist, as the pistol lined up for the kill.

As the dynamometer recorder peaked at 126 mph, Sam felt what little strength he had left flowing from him in a mist of pain. He was finished.

Then suddenly, there was a pungent, piercing smell of aniseed, which even through his pain he knew immediately. The middle cylinder big-end bearing had overheated and set off the stink bomb. Bruno, his senses overwhelmed, let his concentration and his grip slip for a tiny moment, and Sam – knowing full well what would happen next – forced the hand holding the Luger backwards behind a brake cylinder.

On the footplate, they also smelled the big-end warning – and driver Duddington applied the brakes. Instantaneously, as Sam had known it would, the brake cylinder tilted, and above the amazing din he heard the screams as Bruno dropped the gun from his crushed hand. It was all Sam needed. As violently as he knew how, he punched the Nazi on the chin and dislodged him from his precarious position. Slowly but surely, Bruno slid back and sideways, until suddenly he was gone. His screams were enveloped in the cacophony of noises.

On the footplate, oblivious of the drama behind them, the footplate crew congratulated each other in a measured manner, without fuss. Similarly, in the dynamometer car, Sir Nigel Gresley and his team expressed their satisfaction. They had achieved it: *Mallard* had travelled faster than any other steam locomotive in the world.

It was a job well done.

TWENTY THREE

Edgar examined page after page of his *Daily Herald* and looked disappointed. "There's plenty about the record but nowt about thee Sam," he said.

"It was thought best to suppress anything but positive news. No doubt the whole story will come out in the fullness of time," Norman said and smiled.

"Suits me," Sam said. "Job's not done yet."

"What about them? Can you manage?" Edgar asked accepting Norman's statement and Sam's attitude.

"They'll do," Sam said, swinging a heavily-bandaged leg as he balanced on his custom-made crutches.

"What do you mean they'll do?" Edgar protested. "I'm a fitter not a joiner. That's a bloody good job, that is."

Sam grinned in real appreciation. He took clothes from his hospital locker and started to pack his suitcase.

"Your mam and the rest of them'll be here soon," said Edgar.

"That's why I'm leaving now. They'd never let me go."

"Sam, it's less than twelve hours since you were shot!" Edgar still found it hard to take it in.

"And less than two days till I've got to be in

Évian," said Sam, closing the suitcase lid.

Edgar shook his head, and looked at Norman. "I've never known owt like this," he said. "Never."

"Norman's on my side," said Sam. "We've got to leave now to pick up Helena and her dad in London and get the boat across the Channel."

"And what am I meant to tell everybody? God's sake, Sam!"

His brother-in-law laughed. "Back soon, and I'll explain it then. Everything. Come on, Norman."

Norman took the suitcase, and Sam, with the aid of his crutches, made his escape. But only after protestations that he'd not been officially released. It had been a hectic twelve hours.

"I'm glad Herta vouched for me and ended up with Vernon's money," Sam said, as the three stepped into the sunlight where the sports car was parked.

"I'm not sure if she'll be able to keep it all," said Norman. "That's partially up to our man in Berlin who located her."

"Was that difficult?" Sam asked, as Edgar helped him into the car.

"I'm not sure. He moves in curious circles," Norman said. "Strange chap. Likes to wear women's clothes. He says you've met."

Edgar shook his head. He wondered if Sam Bolton would ever be the same again. And only after just one trip abroad …

If you liked Andy's book, you might enjoy *In Too Deep* by Jan Needle, about the disappearance of Buster Crabb, Britain's most famous frogman, during an unauthorised spying mission beneath the first Russian warships to visit Portsmouth Harbour after the war. It is also published by Endeavour.

Extract from *In Too Deep*

IN TOO DEEP

By

Jan Needle

Historical Note

Lionel 'Buster' Crabb was a frogman sent by MI6 — strictly against the orders of the Government — to undertake a top secret mission against a Soviet cruiser bringing two of Russia's most important leaders, Nikita Khrushchev and Nikolai Bulganin, on a 'courtesy visit' to England to ease the growing tensions between the East and West. What exactly happened in the murky depths of Portsmouth Harbour has been declared a secret of the State, bizarrely, for another 40 years.

It was 1956, with the Cold War at a critically fissile stage, but men like Ian Fleming, the naval spy who created 007, and Nicholas Elliott, head of the SIS London Station, were much more gung-ho than their elected masters. Stalwarts of the 'Eton mafia' — rich, young and bursting with self-confidence — they called themselves the Robber Barons.

Unlike Prime Minister Sir Anthony Eden, who had personally forbidden such an expedition, they were sure their plan was brilliant — and fool-proof. They were invincible.

And Buster Crabb was never seen alive again.

One

He was having that dream again. He lay beside her in her comfortable, pristine double bed, and by now it was more like a battlefield. He was a small man, but strong and wiry, and for minutes he had been twisting and writhing like a thing possessed by demons. Pat, as so many times before, did not know what to do.

If she woke him, anything could happen. Once, he had stared at her with eyes filled with rage and hatred, then had thrown himself across the bed at her, one fist drawn back to smash her in the face. She had tried to find it funny that his misjudged momentum had shot him straight off the other side to crash down to the floor. She had failed.

The most frustrating thing was that he would never tell her what the dream was about. She knew it was the same one every time, because some of the words he mumbled or shouted never changed. He was underwater, with a knife, and someone was going to kill him.

Pat Rose had been with him for years now, on and off, and her love was mixed with fear and pity. He would talk about the war in general terms to her, but never on specifics. She had read about him in the papers, though, and in the bar in Chatham where they'd met he was reckoned as a sort of giant. Which considering his stature, struck Pat as endearing; and quite sweet.

He had never claimed himself, even the first time they'd gone to bed together, to be a hero. When she had suggested it, in fact, he'd blushed just like a baby. But he had the George Medal, he admitted, and 'a couple of other stupid gongs' besides. He'd made a croaking noise.

'I'm a frog,' he said. 'That's why I walk so bloody funny.'

'And I'm a barmaid,' Pat returned. 'Ruddy hell, love! You could do better than a skivvy if you wanted to!'

But that, apparently, he could not understand. At first she thought he was putting it on, but he convinced her.

'What you talking about, gal? What's it matter what you work as? Bleeding hell, don't talk so fucking stupid.'

Instead of picking him up on his language, Pat Rose fell in love. She made a noise, Lionel misinterpreted it and apologised for his swearing, and they ended up in a sexy heap. It was the nicest pick-up night she could remember. That either of them could, in fact. And in the first flush of excitement, maybe, he had had no violent dreams.

That had been in Chatham, though, and they lived in London now. Truth is, that was where she'd followed him to, left her home and friends and family. She'd hoped for marriage, and after a while expected it would happen. He was a good man. Kind and generous, and very, very funny.

And he wasn't a wanderer, despite what her girlfriends told her. He was something in the Navy, and of course he had to go off to other places to do work from time to time. Work was like the dreams, though: he wouldn't say exactly what he did. A diver, yeah, a frogman, but so what? The war was over. It was the Fifties. They didn't have an enemy any more.

But he did have secrets, and Pat learned them bitterly. That he drank too much, that he went off with dirty women from time to time, and finally, that he was even married. That had been the bitterest. And wife Margaret was a barmaid too, just like her. Except that she claimed something different now, as did Pat. Pat was a typist by this time, a secretary, she earned a decent wage. She could do ninety words a minute Pitmans.

'And what does she do now?' she screamed, when he admitted that the rumour was correct. 'You bastard, Lionel, you rotten, rotten bastard! I s'pose she's a better class than me, is she? I bet she... I bet she...'

Disarmingly, he'd laughed.

'A better class of barmaid, or a secretary?' he said. 'I 'spect she even gets to put the pencils out!'

Her lips were shaking, and he took her in his arms and embraced her, hard. He was strong, she'd always loved it. And then he coughed, and she coughed, and they shared another fag. His marriage had lasted seven months, he said. It had been another of his big mistakes. A bigger one than usual.

'Like me,' she said. 'Like me, Lionel. Like bloody me!'

'I do like you,' he said. 'Despite your bloody language! In fact I bloody love you, Pat, in fact I bloody want to marry you.'

Silence. Her mouth was hanging open, her eyes were huge. What had he said? Had he meant it? Or had he trapped himself?

Well, not for her sake. She wouldn't do that to a man, not ever. She could hope, though. She could hope.

He shrugged. He shook his shoulders. And he coughed.

'Go on, gal. Turn me down, I dare you. Go on Pat. I want to make an honest woman of you. Any chance?'

Oh yes, Pat Rose could hope.

Soon after that they'd sacked him from the Navy,

was how she understood it, although she wasn't sure, she couldn't get the exact truth out of him. He said he lived in a caravan near the diving school in Portsmouth, HMS *Vernon*, most of the time, and he fell out with them because of the officers. Pat had moved to London, and she found a little flat for him, although she'd said he could move in with her if he wanted to. And when he got sick of mooching round near *Vernon* like a tramp, he got a job not far away, with an old friend called Mr Pendock.

'He thinks that I'm some sort of unsung hero,' he told her. 'He thinks the Government've let me down. It's not a great job, he flogs tables and stuff for the coffee bars, but he says do well and I can be a partner one day. He should be so bleeding lucky!'

The timing had been good, though. His ex-diving partner Syd Knowles had also sickened of the way the Navy had treated the old gang, and had become quite bolshie. He owned his own lorry, and hauled rolls of newsprint down from the paper mills in Lancashire for 'the print.' But these days when he came to Fleet Street with a load, he didn't even bother to contact him sometimes. And that was Crabb's fault, too!

'You get yourself a phone, mate, and I'll bloody ring you up. I'm not searching Soho sleazepits for a night-out chasing crumpet with the likes of you.'

'Pat's got a phone. You could ring her, you know.'

'Aye, and you could marry her. That's what you

told the lass you'd do. And you could stop chasing ten-bob tarts an' all. You're bloody past it, mate. Wise up! That woman's worth her weight in gold.'

Looking at his snoring face beside her now, Pat Rose battled with a small despair. She was still in touch with Syd, they had become real friends. Sometimes when he was doing the London run he looked her out, and they had a drink or two in the sort of pub where Lionel wouldn't be, and they told each other things. Communed. Syd was a gentleman, and married to a woman she spoke to on the phone in Lancashire if she was feeling down. Joan. They had children, too. Syd looked out for her.

Children, for Pat Rose, was sadly not a question any more. She would admit to 'nearly forty' and Lionel was a good bit older. Then there was his drinking, and the diabetes, and the asthma. She had joked once that he needed oxygen to just get up the stairs, let alone for swimming underwater, and he had stayed sulking in his little grubby flat for days. He could be touchy sometimes, Lionel. He could get very hurt.

But the real despair was something that she feared was looming up on her. She'd heard from the neighbours that men had come to call, unknown men with classy accents who'd been sniffing round her house, men they thought might be detectives, maybe, or something to do with what was held to be his 'secret life.' However much she scoffed at such rumours, she couldn't still their wagging tongues.

Which was another reason, Lionel claimed, he had to stay away from her place – then burst into his infectious laughter.

'The idea I've got a secret life,' he hooted. 'Ridiculous.'

She did not think it was ridiculous at all. She suspected his whole life was a secret. He'd been to some very funny places. He knew some very funny men.

'I love it here with you,' he said. He held her hand. He looked into her eyes. 'But I need my freedom, Pat, you know that, love. It's more than just a place I kip, my little pad – it's there to keep me safe, it's my sort of refuge. And if you don't like it, love... well...'

This time Pat let Lionel sleep on, as so many times before. The bad dreams had faded, he was at peace again. But she was not, and it was getting harder. She thought that he was keeping something from her, that something bad was going on.

She didn't think that she could stand it too much longer. She wondered how he'd get along without her. When he woke up, maybe she'd kick him out. She meant it.

Two

Lionel Crabb could dream in cars as well as in Pat's bed, and a few days later his brain raised up the demons as he jounced drunkenly home from Soho in an early morning taxi. This time the dream involved Syd Knowles, and it was split between the warm black Mediterranean and the chilly waters round Portsmouth and the Isle of Wight.

The details, and the sense of terror, were as fluid as the running tide, and the timescale came and went in giant swoops, from wartime till the present day. Sometimes he was dressed in Navy issue overalls, baggy and waterlogged, sometimes in a skintight rubber suit like an Italian, svelte and virile. Likewise his feet: at moments in flexible long fins, at others battered plimsolls, weighted with lumps of lead.

In the Med, where he had started diving, he had sported a long, twisted, deadly knife when underwater, while Syd had favoured a shorter dagger. Neither of them had had to kill with it, although they had been trained to do so, but each could prise off or disable limpet mines. On land, in messes at Gib or Leghorn or Malta, his knife had transformed itself into a stick, hand-made by an Arab craftsman, with a highly- polished cane, and silver hilt engraved elaborately with a golden crab.

In this dream, now, as the squeaky Austin taxi bounced along the tired, rutted roads of post-war London, he relived the last dive the men had done together. It had been a year ago and Syd Knowles had only got it thanks to him. It had been a Navy Intelligence commission, and the cheapskates had figured it could be a one-man job, as befitted peacetime. Two hundred quid to Crabb, and pay his own fares down to Pompey. He had been outraged.

'Bollocks to that,' he'd said to Sydney. 'You still got your lorry, mate? Pick me up in London, take us both down to *Vernon* – they'll organise the gear for us – and afterwards we'll go out on the bash, okay? I'll buy your petrol and forty bars on top. How does that sound?'

'Diesel,' said Syd. 'It's not a bleeding Morris Minor. And how much are you getting for the job, you tight sod?'

'It's fifty five, and five more for my trouble, son. Would I do you down?'

'Aye, you would. You'd screw your dear old bloody mother. Never mind. I'll do it. What's the job?'

On paper, it had been easy. A piece of piss, a cakewalk. There was going to be a fleet review, and the Russians had been persuaded to come and fly the flag. Officially they were allies; they'd helped us win the war, ha bloody ha. The world was nuclear these days, and the Reds were faced up to the Yankees across what Churchill called the Iron Curtain. One false move and World War Three would start.

The Russkies were only sending one big ship, though, a cruiser called the *Sverdlov*. As a threat to a modern navy not a threat at all, although you wouldn't say that to an Ivan, would you? Navy Intelligence claimed she could manoeuvre a bit too smartish for an old design, and maybe had some underwater mods. Syd and Lionel Crabb were going to take a little look.

On paper it was easy, but in real life horrible. The water was full of muck and rubbish, and it was nighttime and the tide was running hard. Syd Knowles was knackered – he'd driven down from Blackburn via London – and Crabbie was half- pissed. They'd both got a bollocking off the officer from *Vernon* who thought he was in charge, and they'd both reacted badly. Divers had their own code. They didn't get pushed around by jumped-up Sawdust Samsons who knew three-fifths of bugger all.

Worst of all, in Crabbie's taxi dream, the horrors seized him by the throat underneath the bulging belly of the *Sverdlov*, and almost killed him. The South Coast tide transformed into the freezing winter waters off Gibraltar, and two Italians came from nowhere, fast and agile in their skin-tight suits and fins. And Syd was gone, Syd Knowles who had been at his side, another hapless Briton in his baggy overalls and pumps. The amateurs. The warriors dressed up as dustbin men.

It was not real, though, and as Syd swam back into his view – the real Syd Knowles, his mate, in the real frogman gear the boffins had copied off the Eyeties – Lionel twisted a valve and injected a blast of pure oxygen into this mouth and lungs. His head cleared, and they saw a cavity in the bottom of the Russian cruiser. A mystery cavity. Had Navy Intelligence been right? Had they struck gold?

Not a lot. In the increased rushing of the ebb, getting low on oxygen, expending muscle-energy hand over fist, they crawled into the cavity and discovered zilch. Maybe the outer hatchway of an airlock frogmen might use for exit and ingress, but

maybe just a rusted, useless bit of hull. They were getting sick of it, and exhausted. And Lionel wanted liquor – badly.

He was no longer sure if he was still in his nightmare, but everything, in an instant, came to a juddering, swooping halt.

'Come on, mate!' the taxi driver shouted. 'Wakey-wakey, rise and shine! You're home now, Mister. Buckingham bleeding Palace! Oi!'

Crabb, in his snazzy clubbing clothes, almost fell out of the cab into the gutter. But he wasn't that drunk, and the dream was gone. The relief was wonderful. As the fare was only eight and six he gave the man a ten-bob note, and waved away the change. He'd had a good night. It all came back to him. He'd won £12 and he'd even got a little feel off Gaynor. And he hadn't drowned...

It wasn't far to his front door, but he had a bit of trouble with the key. Inside, he breathed the smell of home without much pleasure, and grabbed the newel post before tackling the stairs. Maybe he was that drunk. Maybe he was getting past it, like Pat had said.

There was a new smell, though, a different one, and he knew immediately he was not alone. He heard a noise above him. A creak; the sound of breathing. Jesus! Someone had broken in.

Crabb was a short man, but he wasn't short of courage. He favoured tweed suits, a waistcoat and a monocle, and of course the smart cane with crustacean handle. And beneath the handle, his secret weapon. It was a swordstick.

No need to whip the blade out yet. He pushed himself upright, reached for the light switch in the dark, and flicked it on. At the stair-top there was a human being.

'You bastard!' bellowed Lionel Crabb. 'You've taken on more than you can chew this time! Just show your bloody self and die!'

The intruder, bathed in light, looked alone and

vulnerable. No gun, no club, no knife. And he was in a suit, well-cut, dark blue.

'Eh up,' he said, mildly. 'How goes it, flower? I think they've got a little job for you. Are you up to do a lickle bit of swimming?'

'Syd, you bastard!' Crabbie said. 'You'll give me bleeding kittens. What the bloody hell?'

Pat had been right. There was something funny going on.

Three

Unlike Lionel Crabb, Knowles had kept in contact with the secret services, working on the theory they might want to use him for something, some day. Although he found the top men vile, he couldn't get enough of them – even their accents fascinated him. They laughed at his quite openly, because he came from Blackburn, while to him they were like parrots in a farting festival.

Also unlike Crabbie, Syd thought of the main chance. He'd worked his arse off to get his own lorry, and all the hours known to God to make a living in the haulage trade. Not unusual after the war, because the scrapyards were full of ex-Army wagons, and some could be picked up for a song. Some didn't last long and some were death-traps but Syd was a good mechanic. He chose a Bedford, and later upgraded to an ERF with a Gardner engine. He loved it.

So when the cloak-and-dagger boys needed him, they found him easily – they had his number. The call came from the office of Nick Elliott, the London station chief for MI6. A hard-voiced woman told Syd curtly, 'you don't need to know my name,' and demanded to be put in touch with Buster Crabb.

'Buster what?' said Syd, offended. 'Ain't never

heard of him. That's a funny sort of name, chook.'

The 'chook' caused total outrage. He could almost hear her anger rising down the phone.

'Excuse me!' she said. 'Do you know to whom you're talking? Do you have any idea at all?'

'Do I buggery,' he said. 'Do you?'

'I beg your pardon! I most certainly do not!'

'So sod off then, you cheeky bitch. Buster bloody Crabb, my bloody arse.'

He put the phone down in its cradle and smiled across the living room at his wife.

She shook her head.

'You never learn do you?' she said. 'Of course she knows. She rang you up, you

pillock! You'll get in trouble one day, you will.' She laughed.

'You're funny though, I will say that. Who were it?'

'Some stuck-up tart sniffing round for Crabbie. If it's urgent they can try again, so sod 'em. I think I'd better warn Pat though, don't you?'

He thought he wouldn't mention it to Crabb, though. Crabb was bored to death of civvy life, and if the call could get him out of flogging furniture, he'd jump at it.

Which might well be the bloody death of him.

Printed in Poland
by Amazon Fulfillment
Poland Sp. z o.o., Wrocław